AMSTERDAM OCCULT SERIES

BOOK 1

<u>WOLF ANGEL</u>

AMSTERDAM OCCULT SERIES

BOOK 1

WOLF ANGEL

By Mark Hobson

With kind wishes,

from Mark Hobson.

Book cover design by Creative Covers

DEDICATION

This one is for Bruce, Paul and Zia.
The Three Musketeers.

TABLE OF CONTENTS

KONINGSBOSCH VILLAGE - NOVEMBER 1945

He waited until twilight before making the final scurrying dash across the flat field. It just wasn't worth the risk, even with the low concealing mist that seemed to always cover the countryside at this time of the year. Not after the long weeks of hiding and scavenging and sleeping out in the open, all through the summer and into the autumn, moving only at night to avoid the patrols that criss-crossed the area. To blow it all now at the last moment would be devastating.

So he remained sheltered in the undergrowth at the edge of the wood, lying on his stomach, watching the grey building through the gloom.

Way back in March and soon after they had left the devastated ruins of the German city of Aachen, he and the other members of the team had split up and gone their separate ways. Initially they had planned to remain together and if possible to make their way back to Schloss Hulchrath. But the stupid girl had triggered a tripwire, badly injuring her leg and blowing away the face of the boy they called Sepp, killing him. So they had left her crying in the mud with barely a glance back as they hurried away.

A mile or so further on he, the leader, told them that from here on it would be best for each of them to travel alone, to try and make their separate ways back to friendly lines. So after quick handshakes and whispered words of good luck, they had each parted company with the knowledge that they would in all likelihood never see one another again.

He had decided to head west. Resorting to PLAN B like this was not necessarily a bad thing, at least not from his point of view, for he had a firm destination in mind, a place that the others were not privy to. A location which might ultimately be his ticket out of the whole mess that Europe had become. With the war all but lost, and with the Reich's enemies closing in from all sides, he had desperately needed an escape route and as far as he was concerned it was a case of every man for himself.

But what should have been a journey of a few days under normal circumstances had turned into a slow, nerve-wracking trek across war-ravaged Germany of first weeks, and then months. Moving in short stages mostly at night to avoid detection, and scavenging food here and there, stealing from farms or killing the odd rabbit, he had grown physically and mentally exhausted, forever cold even through the summer, and constantly on edge from fear of discovery and most likely death by firing squad. From leaving Aachen in March he had travelled across the border into the southern tip of Holland, taking over eight months to traverse the region. And the war in the meantime had drawn to its final brutal conclusion, with humiliating defeat for the Fatherland giving him added motive to push on. Until finally, on this cold and wet and foggy day in November, he arrived on the outskirts of the small hamlet of Koningsbosch, a dreary and cheerless place in the middle of nowhere, a spot all-but-forgotten by the great events taking place over the last six years. But not forgotten by him.

He'd visited the place on a number of occasions over the years, under orders to carry out periodical checks to make sure that all was in order… just in case it became necessary. His superiors insisted that their plan would be to the benefit of all of Germany, not just during the terrible sacrifices the nation and its people were having to make now, but also for the future generations to come. And knowing what he knew, about the secrets revealed to him during his long stay at

Schloss Hulchrath, he knew that this was no idle boast. In fact the responsibilities placed on him, in the event of the war being lost, were both frightening and thrilling.

So he had endured the hardships and dangers of his long journey stoically, feeling no self-pity or anger. Just a determination to see this through, knowing that this clandestine visit – dangerous though it may be – would place him at the centre of this most secret of operations.

Eventually the late afternoon drew in and the light slowly seeped out of the grey sky, until he decided it was safe to leave his hiding place. Rising slowly into a crouch he slung his small knapsack onto his back and pulled his cap down tight over his blond hair, then cautiously moved forward across the large field. Towards the old stone building that marked the edge of the tiny hamlet, its buttressed walls and small spire just a dark shadow in the damp fog.

Carefully he approached the ancient convent.

The Sisters of the Precious Blood was how they referred to themselves. An Order of cloistered nuns living a peaceful existence in war-torn Europe, in a cold and uninviting building on the outskirts of this tiny, backward community.

It really was the perfect hiding place. The war had mostly passed the place by even though the border with Nazi Germany was just a few miles to the east. The flat and featureless landscape, which was constantly buffeted with cold winds and driving rain, held no attraction or strategic importance to anybody, either to the occupying German forces or later to the American and British liberators. It was a tiny and forgotten part of the country in the very south of Holland in a region remarkably bland. Where people kept to themselves and minded their own business. An ideal location.

He approached the building's heavy wooden door set back into its stone porch, the overhead lamp leaking a feeble glow, and after one final furtive glance around, he banged on the dark surface with the flat of his hand.

There was no movement or sound from within. Which wasn't really surprising. Even with the war over, late-night callers to a convent full of quivering, nervous nuns would set many a heart to beat that little bit faster. So he knocked once more, just that little bit louder and more insistent.

After several minutes he finally heard the scraping of bolts being drawn back and the turning of a key in the large and rusty lock, before the large door was slowly opened several inches and a small and pale face peered cautiously out.

Removing his cap and allowing a small smile to flit across his thin lips, he nodded politely.

"Good evening Reverend Mother"

There was a moment's hesitation as the elderly woman facing him ran her gaze over his features, her eyes narrowing as she attempted to recall who he was, before recognition filtered through. The tiny shiver of fear that caused her lower lip to tremble was only slight, but it was there nevertheless, and when she spoke her voice mirrored her dread.

"Doctor, we were not expecting you."

He simply nodded, said "no", and brushed by her through the entranceway.

Inside the main hall he paused and glanced around, noticing two more younger nuns peering at him through the gloom before they quietly slipped through a doorway and disappeared from view. To his left stretched a long corridor where a third person stood holding a lantern, another novice nun of perhaps fifteen or sixteen, looking at him curiously. He ignored her and turned back to the elderly lady as she re-joined him, having closed and locked the heavy door.

"Mother Annette, I trust you and your charges are all well?"

"Why yes. The year draws to a close and the nights darken, but we are all well."

"Mmm, let us hope this winter is not as severe as last year."

4

"A severe winter it was sir," she agreed, then added, "but with our terrible struggles behind us we all prey for times of hope and reconciliation."

"Yes, quite." He moved forward several steps and glanced once more down the long passageway. "I do apologize for this unannounced visit, and at such a late hour. I hope I have not alarmed you or the young ladies." He again allowed a brief smile at the young nun who was still keeping watch. "However, it is somewhat urgent and my time is short."

"We are always content to welcome you here, at your convenience."

He turned to look squarely at her, unsure whether her words were heartfelt, but dismissed the doubt from his mind. Reverend Mother, or Mother Superior as was her formal title, had always been hard to read and he had precious little time to concern himself with this at the moment. Instead he asked in crisp tones: "Perhaps I could visit your other guests?"

Mother Annette, her elderly face lined and her rheumy eyes downcast, merely nodded.

She led the way into the convent, taking the lantern off the young girl who trailed on behind them both. As he strode down the passageway, which was dark and lined with closed doors and scuttling insects, he noted with a hint of amusement how Mother Annette cast a frightful sight. With her long and dark habit brushing the floor she appeared to glide across the stone flags like a levitating ghost.

At the end of the long passageway they turned right and moved forward into a larger, open space, before angling towards the corner and passing through another doorway. Here there was a stone spiral staircase which he knew led up to the nuns' bare and tiny cells, each simply furnished with a wooden cot and straw mattress, perhaps with a single chair and porcelain wash basin on a side table, and a wooden cross affixed to the wall. But they did not head upwards. Instead they went down.

Twisting deeper and deeper, the three of them stepped down into the shadowy staircase, with the orange glow from the lantern offering scant illumination so that it was necessary to tread carefully on the steps worn smooth from age. At the bottom was another passageway, but this one wide and short. Two doorways led off the central space, one of which was open and revealed a cell set aside for sick or ill residents. Just outside this door was a small stool and desk, and here the young novice nun sat demurely, her eyes still following him with fascination.

Mother Annette led him to the other, closed door.

Taking a hold of the old, iron ring pull, she twisted and then pushed open the solid door, which scraped and shuddered over the uneven stone floor. She did not enter but quickly passed him the lantern and stepped back and turned her face away from the stench that wafted from the room beyond.

Unfazed by the smell, the blond-haired man crossed the threshold, a shiver of excitement passing through him.

Inside the chilly and windowless room he raised the lantern and slowly turned around, the light shivering and sliding across the bare walls. Spaced evenly about the floor were perhaps twenty or so small wooden cribs. Each one had a tiny bundle of blankets within, and tiny pink fingers and heads. Mostly boys he knew, but a few girls as well. Kept here in this secret orphanage.

He smiled in wonder at the beautiful sight, moved almost to tears.

Placing the lantern onto the stone floor he shrugged off the small knapsack and opened it, and reaching inside, he withdrew a long and slender object that glinted in the light as he pulled it free. A noise made him look up again, one of the babes gently sighing in its sleep, perhaps disturbed by the newcomer. The sound filled him with pride.

In a small voice he whispered into the dark. "Hello my young wolves"

After a moment of quiet, and with a feeling of perfect serenity, he turned and passed back through the doorway with the sharp knife held before him.

CHAPTER 1

AMSTERDAM RED LIGHT DISTRICT
MIDNIGHT

The first thing that popped into Inspector Pieter Van Dijk's head as he surveyed the scene was: **Mary Kelly, Miller's Court, Whitechapel, 1888.**

He stood just inside the glass door alongside the strategically placed wall mirror, partly because this was about the only bit of the room's floor that wasn't bloodstained, and also because having walked into the room unprepared he'd found himself suddenly frozen immobile.

For about sixty seconds he reckoned he didn't blink, or breathe. He just looked across at the small bed. And then, as was always the case, he felt ashamed and he briefly looked sideways at his own reflection in the mirror.

Noises of merriment drifted in from outside as another group of tourists flocked by, laughing and enjoying their night out, and he suddenly remembered that he hadn't drawn the curtain across the door behind him. Quickly, and preying none of the gawkers had glanced through the glass, he reached back with his hand and grabbed the red material and yanked the curtain closed, pissed with himself.

Then he turned his gaze back towards the body. *I'm sorry*, he thought, *whoever you are.*

The room was red. Partly from the red neon lights that surrounded the glass entrance, partly from the red frame of the ceiling mirror. But

7

mostly because of the blood, which completely covered the bedsheet and its paper covering, blood so voluminous that it had splashed in waves over the edge of the mattress onto the cheap laminate wood flooring and then spread further, to the very edges of the small room. More red gore had turned the walls crimson, had also fountained upwards to splash and saturate the overhead mirror. It dripped from the small lampshade on the bedside table, surrounded the overturned stool that rested on the floor beside the doorway. And at the centre of it all, the pile of human remnants on the bed itself, legs spread and arms flung to the side, with the torso fully opened up and emptied of its contents – eviscerated was probably the correct medical term, he told himself.

Whoever had done this had really gone to work.

The only other person in the room with him was a fellow cop, Sergeant Daan Beumers, who for once was unusually subdued, which was unnatural for somebody who normally never stopped yakking. He'd been standing at the foot of the bed, bending forward at the waist in order to get a good view of the steaming cadaver, but now his freckled and fresh-faced colleague moved towards him.

"You'd better put these on boss," he said, holding out a pair of plastic galoshes. "I always carry a few spare with me."

As Pieter bent to fit them over his shoes his mind was already starting to slip into gear, going through the priorities: secure the scene – mark a path of contamination to keep the forensic boffins happy – note any smells apart from those emanating from the deceased, such as aftershave, fast food etc – initiate a preliminary survey – evaluate physical evidence possibilities. This was called crime scene management. Later, once the forensic guys arrived other tasks to complete would be to capture the scene photographically – prepare a crime-scene sketch (yes, they still did that, even in the modern age) - retrieve and secure forensic evidence – conduct a search pattern (in this case a radial search pattern centred on the bed would be best) – collect tissue and liquid samples, hairs and fibres, biological samples such as faeces and vomit and semen, DNA and fingerprint gathering – and retrieval of drugs and drug paraphernalia. Next it would be the removal of the cadaver (just how the hell they would do that did nor bare thinking about) and transportation to the lab for the autopsy, where the whole sequence would be repeated again in a much more sterile environment. There was a lot of work to be done, much of it to be carried out immediately by himself and Beumers before the boffins arrived. So best get on with it.

Pieter slid and squelched his way towards the bed, and turned his clinical cop's eyes onto the victim before him.

It never ceased to amaze him of the kind of damage that could be done to the human body, both before and after death. Gunshot wounds resulting in fatalities were becoming more frequent in the city, especially those involving criminal gangs whose main illegal trade involved drug smuggling and people trafficking, but in a country where the acquisition of firearms was still quite difficult due to the stringent gun-ownership laws the main cause of death in murder cases was from stabbing. These usually involved a small number of wounds to the front of a person's torso or defensive cuts to the palms and fingers. But even a single stab could be enough to leave frightful injuries, the insertion and retraction of a blade ripping through skin, tendons and if deep enough nicking bones and piercing organs. The loss of blood could be either minimal or plentiful, but other 'substances' could be released, such as bizarre-looking bulges of flesh protruding through the openings, bone fragments, urine or faeces if the blow was to the bladder or intestines, not to mention brain-matter or teeth or ocular fluid if the trauma was to the head. Other weapons, such as blows from an axe or machete or screwdriver for example, left a variety of types of injuries, just of a bigger nature. And over the years working as a murder cop, Inspector Van Dijk thought he had seen pretty much everything there was to see when it came to murder. But looking closely at the corpse on the bed he realized that this murder was basically off the scale.

The pair of them worked diligently and efficiently, moving around the scene as little as possible but determined to be a thorough as they could, as they both had an unspoken understanding that this murder was unlike anything that either of them had worked before. Having worked as a team for nearly three years now they intuitively understood one another and this past experience had turned them into a well-oiled machine, and they each in turn recorded their observations or pointed out certain injuries – the obvious opening-up of the abdomen from the sternum down past the vagina – the removal of the intestines and certain organs like the uterus and kidneys – the severance of the right carotid artery, with blood splattering's on the wall to the right side of the bed supporting this – the position of the body, which was lying flat on her back but with the axis of her body inclined to the left, with her left arm stretched out towards the panic-button on the wall. Other observations included the careful parting of large flabs of skin from the costal arch to the pubes, with both sides peeled back and folded across the mattress, revealing the ribcage, with parts of the spine showing through the empty cavity where the organs had been removed. The face was cut with multiple lacerations to the cheeks, forehead and eyes, and the nose had been sliced off. Both legs were open with the knees bent and the soles of the victim's feet flat against the mattress, and both legs had deep wounds on the inner thighs and calves.

They worked with their minds switched on to the task at hand but with their personal thoughts and natural revulsion temporarily held in check, and just as they were finishing with this initial survey of the crime scene they both heard a gentle tapping on the glass door behind them. Sergeant Beumers moved across and lifted the edge of the curtain to see who was standing outside.

"Ah, it's Tweedledum and Tweedledee, the jizz squad," he remarked, before opening the door to let the two forensic technicians slip inside.

Fully suited and booted in their white paper hooded coveralls and surgical mouth coverings, both nodded hello to the pair of cops before one of them griped, "for God's sake, who the hell has been walking all through the blood? Don't you guys ever listen? When I say don't disturb the crime scene I mean stay the hell away and let us professionals take over." He looked up from where he'd been scowling at the pools of blood, stared hard at the two officers, before his eyes shifted to look past Pieter's shoulder towards the bed. "Fuck!" he exclaimed.

Pieter and Beumers exchanged a look. "Exactly," Beumers replied.

Moving past the techie, Pieter slapped him gently on the shoulder. "It's all yours".

Then he and Beumers quickly removed their blood-soaked galoshes before stepping outside into the alley, to breath in the relatively clean air.

Trompettersteeg was possible the narrowest and most crooked of alleyways in all of Amsterdam. Barely three feet wide along its whole length, it was impossible to pass another person without turning sideways and squeezing by. Half of its length, at the bottom where it opened out by Gottahaves Coffeeshop onto Oudezijds Voorburgwal canal, was covered over with a brick ceiling, this dark and frightening tunnel covered in graffiti and plastered with flyers. The other end near where they came out onto, which was occupied by around a dozen windows and their girls, and which was the only segment with any lighting, opened out onto a hustling and bustling intersection of other alleys and side streets and the indoor segment of window brothels. The place was hundreds of years old, creepy as hell, and was the heart of the Red Light District. And tonight it was jam packed with tourists and groups of men, all packed in and desperate for a glimpse of the working girls, some drunk or reeking of weed but most of them good-natured and out for a memorable night on the town. Oblivious to the horrors just inches from where they shuffled passed.

With a glance up both lengths of the alley, Pieter turned to the uniformed officer standing guard just outside the glass door of the room they had exited.

"Get rid of all these people will you. Seal off both ends with tape. But don't let any of the other girls leave just yet. Oh, and get the memory cards for the CCTV cameras from the security cabin bchind Durty Nellies pub."

"The girls won't like it. And their pimps will kick off. The girls here charge the highest prices, they can earn a couple of thousand euros each per night," Beumers told him.

"I don't give a fuck. If they don't like it, tell them to contact their union." Pieter nodded at the uniform who scurried off into the shadows.

He stepped back one step until he leaned against the wall opposite the murder scene, looking at the glass door and the red light around the frame.

"Was the light still on when her pimp found her?" he asked Beumers.

"He says he didn't touch anything, so I guess so."

"It must have happened pretty much as soon as her client entered the room then, before they even got down to business." He scratched at his chin, his fingers catching the old scar down the side of his neck. "And something like *that*" he nodded at the door "would take some considerable time. Not a quick kill and a rushed getaway. What exactly did her pimp have to say?"

Beumers shrugged his shoulders. "Not a lot. Claims she was with the John for a long appointment, and he didn't like to disturb them, and then says he fell asleep watching TV. Which is crap as you know. Whether they pay the usual fifty euros or pay three hundred euros, they want them to fuck the girl fast and then piss off. Mind you, he was watching La La Land so perhaps he is telling the truth and nodded off half way through."

"Really?"

"Really."

"What about the other girls down here?"

"Well I've only had a quick chat with a few," Beumers told him, "but surprise surprise they all claim to have seen or heard nothing."

"Nobody? They have mirrors by the side of their doors so they can see men coming up and down the alley. I thought these girls were supposed to look out for one another?"

"Yeah well boss, they all say they were in the toilet at the time, or some such shit."

Pieter watched as a couple of uniformed officer's started to marshal the crowds of tourists out of the alley. At the top end, another forensic techie came down the alley with several camera bags slung around his neck.

"Well speak to them all again. And get their contact details. I'll get some of the lads to help out because the girls will be changing shifts in a few hours."

The camera guy stopped before them. "This one?" he asked, pointing at the door.

Pieter and Beumers nodded at the same time, and he stepped inside. The door shut and after a moment the two of them heard his muffled "Fuck me" come from within the room.

Just then the police officer he'd sent away to tape off the exits came rushing back towards them, looking flustered. "Sir, there's something you gotta see."

He led them down towards the darker end of the alley, where the walls closed in even more, and the old brickwork was covered in scrawled messages about HIV and flyers about illegal raves, calling back over his shoulder excitedly, "I saw it when I came down… just before the end here… I could have walked right by it, but I didn't."

He paused, and fished out his mobile from his back pocket, and turned on its bright white light, and held it up high at arm's length to shine it on the wall at head height. To show this:

Beware, Werewolf is watching

It was daubed in red, presumably with blood as the writing was starting to congeal and turn a darker rust colour.

Beumers glanced sideways at him. "What are you thinking boss?" he asked.

Pieter stared with hard flinty eyes up at the wall. "What am I thinking? I'm thinking why didn't I just get a job working at KFC when I left school?"

He turned as if to move away, out of the exit of the passageway.

"Where are you going now?"

Turning to look back over his shoulder, Pieter told him simply, "Danny boy, I'm off to get a beer."

CHAPTER 2

LOTTE

The Newcastle Bar over on Oudezijds Achterburgwal canal was a bit of a dive. The owner must have been a surfer at one time, thought Pieter, even though the best place for surfing in the Netherlands was way over at Zandvoort on the North Sea coast. Like most surfer's shacks, the place was run-down and dingy, with wooden planks for walls and rickety bar stools and bare floors covered in gum, with a multitude of optics and beer pumps behind the bar and the ceiling plastered with currency notes from all parts of the world, US Dollars, Japanese Yen, South African Rand, British Sterling, Swiss Franc and so on, and one whole wall made up of postcards and photos tacked over every square inch. The toilet, which was tiny and unisex and with no lock on the door, was a breeding ground for every deadly microbe known to man, and it never flushed and the sink gurgled brown water back *up* the plughole. Also the place was tiny, and with window brothels to either side of the barn-door entrance it tended to attract characters of a shady nature.

But Pieter liked it here.

There was something about the edgy atmosphere that seemed to appeal to him. Perhaps it was because people tended to mind their own business and ignored the dodgy dealings going down, the patrons content to sit and stare into their glasses, their eyes flicking left and right whenever anybody pulled up a stool or stumbled past as they rushed outside to puke into the canal.

Yes, it was that kind of joint.

And of course Lotte worked here.

From Finland, and in her early twenties, and on a gap year from Uni to do a bit of travelling, before ending up in Amsterdam and getting this cash-in-hand bar job, which was two years ago now, and what had initially been planned as a short stay had become a semi-permanent home.

Pieter had called in one day to have a quick drink on his way home from work and had noticed the new bar girl, who had drifted across to where he was sat at the end of the bar and smiled shyly at him, head tilted to one side to ask what she could get him.

"Heineken please."

Watching her as she drew the beer into a chilled glass, she aware of his friendly scrutiny but a little too timid to glance across and make eye-contact, but playing with a strand of hair and twisting it behind one ear, then bringing his drink over and scooping off the frothy head with a knife, pretending to concentrate on what she was doing but Pieter noticing her swift glance towards his hand and noticing the wedding ring he wore. Then another sweet little smile. "I'm Lotte," she had quietly told him, before moving away to serve another customer. Pieter smiling.

Their first introduction.

He stayed to have another beer. He told himself it was because of the hot summer weather and his long, tiring day at the station, but he knew it was really because he wanted her to serve him again just so their little encounter could happen again. And he'd found himself asking himself *what the heck? Aren't you a little old to become besotted with the new girl behind the bar?* But then he'd glanced down towards where she was standing by the till and caught her peeking at him from the corner of her eye, and he had given a little laugh and she had given a little laugh and everything was good.

So from then on Pieter had popped in once or twice a week, especially after his divorce finally came through, usually in the evenings when he knew she'd be here, and although they'd never dated or anything and only ever saw each other here in the bar, he was sure that each time he walked through the entrance her face would light up when she saw him arrive. It was a cool and lovely friendship, both of them really enjoying each other's company, for he soon discovered after breaking through her natural shyness she was quite possibly the sweetest person he'd ever known.

Sitting here now, at a little after one in the morning and coming from the horror of the murder scene, he was in dire need of hearing her soft voice and seeing her little gestures, the touch of her fingers on his hand as she talked freely, bringing him up to speed on her day.

At the moment she was busy with a large group of backpackers who had put in a big order, and she was rushed off her feet pouring a glass of this and a glass of that, and so she glanced down towards him and pulled a face and raised her eyebrows and whispered *sorry.*

While he waited he watched the soccer on the TV above the bar, vaguely listening to two drunken Irishmen trying to pluck up the courage to go and see one of the girls in the windows next door.

He was pretty sure that, apart from Lotte, nobody who frequented the bar knew he was a cop, not even the bar owner, a fat bloke called Bart. He preferred it that way. Not because he liked to be incognito, surreptitiously listening in to people's conversations, constantly on the lookout for any collars he could feel. No, when he called in for a drink and a chat, he was strictly off-duty, and didn't care less for the low-key illegal activity that might be playing out around him. Short of actually witnessing a murder Pieter was more than happy to turn a blind eye to the pub's varied patrons and their comings and goings.

Lotte eventually broke away from the other end of the bar and sashayed towards him mischievously.

"Hey"

"Hey" he smiled back, the weariness in his body temporarily lifting.

"The usual?"

"Best make it a large one"

Lotte stuck out her bottom lip. "That kind of day?"

"Aren't they always?"

She poured his beer, looking up at him through her blonde fringe. "I heard there was something bad going on over behind the church. Half the place cordoned off."

"Yep I just came from there." He sipped at his drink, sighing as the cold liquid hit the spot.

"There's all kinds of rumours going around. A shooting, or possibly a tourist getting stabbed. Very gory they say."

"News travels fast"

"But then Bart, he told me he was heading down Sint Annenstraat on his way here, and there was all kinds of chaos in the next street over, shouting and stuff, so he cut through to have a look, and he said this guy, who he thought was one of the pimps, he was puking up all over the place, and so Bart says it must be one of the girls." Lotte looked at him closely. "Is it one of the girls?" She shuddered at the thought.

"Ah, you know what Bart's like, full of crap most of the time"

Lotte didn't seem to hear him. She was just shaking her head and saying "poor thing" to herself.

Over near the door the two Irish blokes were having a whispered conversation and counting out their euro notes. Then one of them slipped away, sliding around the door with his collar turned up. His buddy returned to his seat, had a sip from his glass, and then continued tallying up his money. Pieter turned back to Lotte.

"Do you think it's the same person who killed that girl a few years ago?" she was saying. "The police never caught anyone for that. What was she called?"

"Berti. But I don't think so. That was a good few years ago now, and her killer will be long gone. He was probably on a plane at Schiphol before her body was even discovered."

"So it is another girl then?" She looked at him earnestly.

Pieter couldn't help but smile, for he knew her concern was genuine. "Have you ever considered switching careers?" he joked.

Lotte grinned back. "And miss working here? In this classy establishment? Serving all of these sweet people living on the fringes of society?"

"Present company excepted," Pieter pointed out.

"I didn't say that." With a wink, Lotte scooted off to see to another customer.

Pieter took a long sip of beer, which helped to banish thoughts of the murder scene and further settled his head. He knew from experience that the next few days would be full-on unless they made an early arrest, and so this quick visit to catch up with Lotte was akin to the calm before the storm, a last piece of normality before the work began in earnest tomorrow.

He was just reaching out for his glass once more when he felt his mobile vibrate against his thigh, and so he reached into his trouser pocket, seeing he had a text message from Daan Beumers.

INITIAL ID ON THE GIRL – WORKING NAME OF MILA. REAL IDENTITY NEVER ESTABLISHED BY HER PIMP. HE THINKS SHE COMES FROM ESTONIA, BUT NOT 100% SURE. CLAIMS NOT TO HAVE HER PASSPORT. NOW HE IS OVER THE SHOCK HE'S COMING OVER AS A MOUTHY CUNT, BUT MY GUT FEELING IS THAT HE'S IN THE CLEAR. EVEN THE BEST ACTOR IN THE WORLD CAN'T THROW UP ON DEMAND THE WAY HE WAS. ENJOY YOUR BEER BOSS.

Pieter put the phone away and finished his drink.

CHAPTER 3

DAD

On sunny days during the spring or at weekends, Pieter liked to walk along De Ruijterkade by the side of the river Ij, to visit his dad. The stroll took him by the large and luxurious riverboat cruises moored to the west of Centraal Station, and then on beyond the up-market yacht marina, before he came to the old decrepit boathouses moored at the riverside. Most were unseaworthy with leaking old hulls, their sides lined with old tyres to prevent them bumping and rubbing against one another, but a few of the nicer ones had been turned into cute little floating cafes permanently moored up alongside the railings.

His dad lived in one of the smaller ones right at the end of the line, the one with the blackened chimney on its flat roof, with smudges of wood smoke drifting out. Despite Pieter's protestations, his dad still enjoyed taking his floating home out onto the river to do a spot of fishing from time to time, even though Pieter was convinced that one day the thing would end up at the bottom of the riverbed, the two old wrecks sharing a watery grave.

On occasion the two of them would head for the Western Islands for an amble around the old boatyards and wooden bridges which was fast becoming one of the up-and-coming parts of Amsterdam to live in. Or perhaps they would go down Singel to pop into Greenwoods English Café close to where Pieter lived.

But today, even though it looked like it was set to be a nice and warm morning, Pieter was in a hurry and so had to call around on a flying visit by car, before doubling back to Police HQ over on Elandsgracht. On his way over he hurried into Albert Heijn, the small spar shop on the corner, to grab a few essentials for his dad.

Parking his car in the parking bay on the far side of the road, Pieter skipped across, avoiding the cyclists scooting by, and bounced his way down the narrow gangplank. He let himself in with his own set of keys, hearing the morning news on the TV before he passed through into the boat's living area.

Dad was up – still in his pyjamas, but at least awake and in the land of the living, which these days was a bonus. He was slouched on the old couch, eating a slice of toasted French bread and drinking coffee.

"Hi pops," Pieter said with a slightly exaggerated gaiety (it was important always to appear positive with dad these days)

"Son," dad mumbled between bites, nodding at the TV. "How much do you reckon her teeth cost her?"

Pieter glanced at the glamourous female news-anchor on the TV set, the one his dad had a crush on, the few perks that the randy old goat had. "More than my retirement fund probably," he replied, stepping across to the kitchen area and taking the eggs, milk and croissants out of the carrier bag, noticing when he opened the fridge that dad was low on appelstroop. As he unpacked, he glanced down the narrow corridor towards the small bedroom at the end, seeing that the door was open. It seemed that Famke, dad's lady friend, wasn't around, which was always a relief. Famke, who was around about sixty he thought, although her wrinkled and haggard face made her appear much, much older, was a bad influence. Like his dad, she was an alcoholic, and although his dad was currently on the wagon having her about the place regularly was sometimes too much of a temptation for his old man. Their friendship was a sore point between father and son, and had resulted in too many blazing rows, but dad insisted on letting her pop over and occasionally staying the night. But thankfully there was no sign of her today.

Pieter went back into the living area and handed the morning paper to his dad. Hansje turned straight to the sports page, a lit cigarette now in his mouth, checking the soccer results and grumbling, ash spilling down his pyjama top. Pieter noted the ashtray, which was one of those cheap plastic ones that his dad had stolen from a pub years ago, was filled to overflowing.

Standing there and looking around at the mess, the threadbare rug and the dying plants, the plate of half-eaten supper from the night before on the coffee table, the grimy windows and so on, his dad looking all bony and shrivelled up with his grey hair and stubbly, unshaved chin, Pieter felt an almost overwhelming feeling of sadness. He sagged inside, and a bone-deep weariness of the soul gripped him.

He glanced across to the wall by the small, round porthole, and at the framed photo there. It was a group shot of dad and his army buddies, all proud and healthy men in their uniforms with their blue UN Peacekeeping berets on. The photo had been taken at a Dutch base near the town of Potocari in Bosnia Herzegovina sometime in early 1995.

Just a few months before Srebrenica.

Driving over to the main police headquarters which was situated at the south end of the Jordaan district, Pieter pressed the button that lowered the side-window, the morning breeze ridding his nostrils of the stale smell of dad's place. He drummed his fingers on the steering wheel as he navigated his way slowly through the morning cyclists and trams.

Srebrenica. It always came back to Srebrenica.

Pieter had only been around twelve years old at the time, and back then hadn't really known too much about the whole mess. But what he did know was that when his dad had left as part of a six month tour to the hell-hole of war-torn Bosnia his dad had been a happy and carefree person, a loving husband, and the best father in the world. But he had returned a wreck of a man, an empty shell, a weak person who was prone to angry outbursts and bouts of heavy drinking and petty crime. Whatever he'd experienced out there had changed him seemingly overnight, until the boozing and violence first of all ended his marriage, and then for many years drove an irreparable wedge between father and son. He'd been unable to hold down a steady job after leaving the army, had drifted from rented home to rented home, hated everyone and everything around him, resulting in long periods in rehab for the drinking, not to mention a spell in prison for assaulting a gay guy inside Prik Nightclub (dad refused ever to explain why he was there in the first place) For nigh on fifteen years he had drifted through life as a total messed up alcoholic, before finally Pieter and his dad had reconciled following mum's death, and Pieter was at last able to get him the help he needed. But even now, all of these years later, life for the two of them was a constant struggle with Pieter forever on guard for dad's latest relapse (which happened frequently)

But the ghosts from Bosnia never truly left him. It was obvious to Pieter those demons would be an ever-present shadow in both of their lives. Put simply, Srebrenica had seared his dad's soul.

He tried to shake off his melancholic mood about his father by listening to some music on his playlist, and when he finally pulled into the parking spot reserved for him by the side of the police building he had succeeded in putting aside his family concerns, at least temporarily.

Walking around to the front of the large brick building Pieter entered by the main entrance, was buzzed in by the desk sergeant, and then headed up the stairs to the top floor, using his key card at each security door he passed through. Passing the desks in the main squad room Pieter entered his tiny corner office, booted up his PC and made a coffee whilst waiting.

Just as he was sitting down and taking his first sip Sergeant Daan Beumers poked his head around the doorframe. Pieter saw he was still wearing the same clothes from last night. "You want the bad news first, or the even badder news?" he asked.

"Let me guess. Our lottery syndicate came up with a winning number, but you forgot to put it on?"

"I said bad new, not catastrophic news." He moved into the office, lifted a pile of files off the spare chair beside the door and dumped them haphazardly onto the long table in the corner. Beumers sat with a groan, and then fished out a small note book from his breast pocket and flicked to the relevant page. When it came to smart phones or iPads

Beumers was a bit of a wiz, but occasionally he still preferred the old-fashioned methods of being a copper.

"Anyway boss, we still don't have anything concrete on the girl's identity other than what I messaged you last night. Everybody just knew her as Mila. Her pimp did tell us she was 22 years old but the girl in the next door room who was quite close to her has just revealed that she was actually 19, so underage since the law was changed. Also, she'd been working since she arrived from wherever about a year ago, so that makes her even younger when he first pimped her. But it's fairly certain that she's from Eastern Europe. All of the black girls work over past Oude Kerk and all of the trannies tend to congregate across towards Nieuwmarkt. Trompettersteeg is where all the stunners are put, and our Mila was said to be a real looker even by the usual standards in that alley. Not that you could tell last night, obviously," he finished quietly.

Pieter said nothing, just blew across the top of his steaming coffee.

"Anyway, we checked the CCTV," Beumers went on more brightly.

Pieter looked up.

"But the fuckers were switched off. The blokes over at Durty Nellies claim they were down for maintenance – at midnight? – but more likely they were just cutting down on costs as those cams are paid for by the girls' enforcers rather than the coffers at city council. So basically we have nothing on film. And no witnesses, or at least nobody willing to come forward and speak, which is nothing new I guess."

"What about inside the room itself?" Pieter asked quietly, opening up the file from last night's murder on his computer.

"Boss?"

"Hidden cameras placed in her room? Usually right close to the bed? Some of the pimps put them in without the girls and their clients knowing, and they live-stream it over the internet."

"Really? Fuck me. How much does that cost?" Beumers enquired.

"They accept payment by direct debit if you're interested," Pieter told him mischievously. "Anyway, check it out."

24

He leaned forward and started scrolling through the file, quickly skimming the crime scene photos that had been downloaded overnight, until he found the one's of the writing on the wall near the end of the small alleyway. He motioned his colleague across, who came around the desk to get a better look, pocketing his notebook.

"We need to do a database check on this. Run it through ViCASnl to see if any links crop up." He referred to the Netherlands' new police software system, which was a powerful search engine that scoured every police crime report for similarities, whether it be weapons, types of injuries or victims, DNA and fingerprints, messages, vehicle matches, geographical links and a whole gamut of other stuff that the crime eggheads could come up with. ViCASnl stood for Violent Crime Analysis System (Netherlands) and was based on the FBI model, and was a relatively new concept on this side of the Atlantic. Pieter tapped the screen, thinking aloud. "This must mean something to someone," he said, indicating the strange symbol. "And this here," he pointed at the word werewolf in the message, "this suggests one person, the way it's worded – *Beware, Werewolf is watching"* – see if anything gets flagged up."

"How wide a search do you want?" Beumers asked.

"European-wide. Ask our friends at Interpol to run a similar search on their system." He sat back in his chair. "And bring her pimp in. Squeeze his balls and see if he reacts, at the very least he's looking at five years for sex-trafficking and pimping out an underage girl, so see if you can use that as leverage. Also get those CCTV guys over here. It seems just too much of a coincidence that those security cameras were down at the exact time our guy was killing Mila. Either that, or he just had the luckiest break ever."

"You know, I just don't get that," Beumers told him, rubbing the back of his neck to ease the tenseness in his muscles. "Whoever did that to that girl, the stuff we saw, they'd have to be covered head-to-foot in blood. Literally dripping in it. Cameras or no cameras, somebody would have to spot a guy looking all messed like that, running through the streets. The place was packed with people. They'd be a trail of blood leading us right the way to the bastard's front door."

"Yeah. We could put out an appeal for any members of the public to check their mobile phone or camcorder footage, see if anybody caught anything or anyone suspicious. But I don't want to go down that route yet." Pieter hit the print key on the computer to start printing out the crime scene pics. As the printer over on the long table whirred to life he asked: "Was there much on the news today? I wasn't really paying much attention on the way over."

"A brief mention on the local TV channel, but no real details, just that the police are dealing with a suspicious death in De Wallen. Fucking suspicious? More like mysterious."

"Well let's keep things low-key for now. I want to keep that message and symbol as hold-back evidence. Let's just prey no members of the public noticed it amongst all of the graffiti, otherwise all of the crackpot copycats will be busy."

Pieter walked over to the printer and took out the sheaf of papers, and glanced through them with a grimace.

"You know, what you said a moment ago? About the killer been drenched in blood and what he did to her? That to me didn't feel like a first-kill. Most first time murders are fairly mundane, sometimes even accidental. Maybe an argument that went too far, or a crime of passion, perhaps just a single stab wound, before the murderer flees in a panic. But last night, that took time. You'd have to be very cool to spend maybe an hour or two butchering a person like that, knowing there are throngs of people walking past just a few feet away. It certainly doesn't feel like the behaviour of someone taking a human life for the very first time."

Beumers took a moment for the implications of that to sink in. Then he remarked, "yeah, but if that *was* his first victim, what the hell is coming next?"

CHAPTER 4

MR SNAKEHIPS

Oliver Monroe was jiving and jitterbugging his way down Warmoesstraat, feeling like *the man,* and out looking for some pussy to grind. '

Earlier at his hotel, which was conveniently positioned right beside Centraal Station, he had snorted some charlie to help stimulate his libido, and then on the walk over here he had scored a bit of angel dust from one of the tsk tsk drug dealers, sprinkling it on his spliff to inhale the rocket fuel directly into his system. The combination helped to mellow his mind but also to leave him highly sexed up almost to bursting point, and this floaty and disconnected sensation just on the edge of feeling trippy made the night around him dazzle and shine, so that the lights from the bars and the music and chatter pinged around inside his mind, and the paving stones glowed like in the Michael Jackson *Billie Jean* music video.

Oliver was from London, and every two months his work called for a quick flight across to Amsterdam for face-to-face round-table conferences with the execs who paid his wages as a broker. The meetings usually lasted about a couple of hours, short enough for him to catch the evening flight back to Gatwick. However, Oliver always ensued that these trips involved a one-night stopover, which his very generous expenses paid for. And so, after a short call home to the wife in their Maida Vale apartment to assure her how much he loved her and their ten month old baby girl, the evenings inevitably found him out enjoying everything that Amsterdam's infamous nightlife had to offer.

What happened in Amsterdam stays in Amsterdam.

Oliver had visited quite a few of the world's sex capitals. In Bangkok on holiday with his then fiancé, he'd managed to blag an evening by himself once when Jessica had been feeling unwell, and he'd headed straight for the Soi Cowboy district with its notorious girly bars. Naturally he had indulged himself fully (except the pre-teen kiddies, which didn't really float his boat) and had found himself drifting through the streets, the warm and sultry night seeming to add to the sleazy nature of the place, everybody hot and sweaty, his clothes sticking to his body, the girls sitting on his lap and wriggling their cute asses. Years earlier he had gone along on a stag weekend to Ibiza with a bunch of friends from The City, and on both nights they had gone to Space nightclub, the largest nightclub in the world. With its 10,000 person capacity, the drugs and dance music throbbing through his veins, watching the sex show underneath the huge glass-domed roof, he had been buzzing and lusting at the women until seven in the morning. But for him, for the variety of experiences on offer, with every perverted taste catered for, plus the coffee-shops and the stunning-looking girls and the edgy feel to the red light district, nothing quite beat Amsterdam. It was *the* Sin City. And even better, it was only a 45 minute flight from the UK! Perfect for a bit of extra-marital horizontal extra-curricular activity!!

So here he was, jinking and slinking along the street like Mr Snakehips, or strutting like a prize thoroughbred, horny as hell and out to lay waste to this town.

Turning down Lange Niezel, Oliver paused from time to time to look into the sex shop windows, spying the dildos and love dolls and lube cream and anal ticklers and ball-gags, feeling his sexual frenzy start to build and grow, so that by the time he turned right past Oude Kerk and reached the heart of the Red Light District, heading into the maze of narrow alleyways with their red-lit windows, to Oliver it felt like his cock was so gargantuan it seemed like he'd grown an extra leg.

Way to go, baby! He mouthed to the blondes and redheads and brunettes through the glass windows, *wait until you see what I've got for you!!*

Most of the girls ignored his antics, more interested in their mobile phones, which he found fucking annoying. Ok, but not to worry. *Because one of you lucky girls is gonna get the ride of your life. Hubba hubba, cry for your momma! No mercy!!*

Oliver spent about half an hour wandering about and trying to choose a girl, heading into the indoor windows next to La Vie en Proost strip club, and then across the canal to the interconnecting streets between this and the next canal, his eyes ogling every woman he saw, even other tourists that caught his eye, up and down Bloedstraat, Stoofsteeg, Zeedijk. Until finally just around the corner from Sex Shop Caligula he spotted *the* one. A cute and petite brunette, eastern-European by the looks of her features, with a perfect set of tits and a humping perfect body. *Oh la la, you gorgeous fitty,* he nodded to himself, pleased with his choice. And so he stood directly opposite her window, legs apart like the Colossus of Rhodes, just waiting for her to see him and drag him lustily inside.

After a minute, when she failed to glance up from her mobile and notice him, he hopped across and tapped on the glass.

It didn't take long to negotiate a transaction, her with the door open and people walking by listening in. *How much for a suck and a fuck hun? – Fifty euros, or for two positions one hundred euros – ok babe let's party, and make it good ok!!*

Inside it was straight down to business. Money passed hands, off with their kit, a quick wash of his dick over by the bidet, on with the extra-large Johnny ha-ha! And Bob's your uncle before he knew what's what he was banging her doggy style like the end of the world was nigh and she was screaming for mercy like they always do!!

For twenty minutes straight he fucked her like the piece of meat she was, dirty little girl, slutty teeny-bopping whore, my sexy little nympho, Oliver for some reason unable to get the image of his wife out of his mind despite his best effort not to think about her. And just when it looked like the poor girl was about to pass out from exhaustion he finally finished with one last thrust and a slap on her bum for good measure.

Five minutes later and he was back outside, with a huge satisfied grin on his face and still feeling the effects of a cocaine rush. In desperate need of a piss, he headed across the bridge towards the outdoor urinal near Oude Kerk.

As he hurried over the cobbles he glanced at his watch, noticing that it was coming up to two in the morning. Jesus, where did the time go? A good job he'd booked a later flight for tomorrow, he reckoned he could spend another couple of hours here before heading back over to his hotel. Perhaps grab a drink, pop a couple of pills of Bloom, and maybe have Round 2 as he was still feeling randy as hell. Or he could go and watch one of the live sex shows, and maybe get selected for a bit of audience participation, fuck yeah! They might even offer him a job.

Either way the night was still young, and wifey was still waiting back home, convinced that her hard-working husband was tucked up in bed, homesick and counting down the hours until he came dashing through the front door to fling his arms around her and the baby.

Silly bitch. If she'd have tried being a little more adventurous in the bedroom department then perhaps he wouldn't need to get his jollies away from home like this. It wasn't his fault that he was highly sexed and brimming with testosterone. He wanted – no, he needed – sex virtually every night, and if she wasn't willing to provide what he required, then really he had no option but to see all of the escort girls back in the UK or make these trips abroad. And screwing a prostitute wasn't that big a deal these days, at least he wasn't having a proper affair behind her back. So really, when you thought about it, it was really all her fault, and he was the reluctant victim here.

Laughing loudly to himself and the night, Oliver stepped into the outdoor urinal, and started having a good piss.

Yes, it had been a very worthwhile trip. The meeting earlier had been mostly a formality, really just a case of sitting there and letting the execs run through their annual targets and profits threshold, while he, Oliver, had nodded his head and spoke words of praise which always helped to massage their fragile egos. He had even broached the subject of raising his expenditure allowance for these trips, mentioning his excellent record of undercutting their chief rivals and bringing in extra secured assets in the process, oh and by the way I now have a young family and these trips away from home are quite a drain on my private home life and quality time. It had worked a treat, and he'd secured a very satisfying response, and the extra expenditure had nicely paid for the top quality cocaine that he'd snorted earlier.

Standing there and emptying his bladder into the small drain in the ground, with only his upper body and feet visible to any passers-by, Oliver suddenly noticed the quiet that had descended, the streets and canal-side empty of people and noise. At this time of night it was hardly surprising that most of the crowds were gone, the tourists starting to drift away, but there were normally a few people about. Yet at the moment everywhere was still, and a bizarre hush had descended. He glanced around and looked across the small cobbled square next to the church. Oh, there was somebody standing over there after all, noticing two shadowy silhouettes by the wall. And another, this one a little closer up on the bridge to his right. What's more, they seemed to be watching him. Standing stock-still and just staring.

Oliver squinted and tried to make out their faces, but it was impossible to see much in the dark, and anyway, why the hell were they looking at him taking a piss? Were they fucking faggots or something? There were enough of them around, and to each his own, Oliver had no issues with anybody's sexual preferences, but come on! They were putting him off. A man needs his privacy.

Sighing and shrugging in annoyance, Oliver glanced down at his dick and shook off a few drops, and started to zip himself up.

But then there was a sudden rush of footsteps, a scraping of feet on the cobbles close by, and somebody giggling. And the creepy thing about it was that Oliver was convinced it was a child's voice

He felt something weird between his legs, a sudden cool draft around his scrotum and then a wetness that dribbled down his trouser leg.

Silly bugger, he scolded himself, you haven't even finished taking a leak and now you've gone and pissed down your frigging trousers. But the wetness didn't trickle away, it actually became a sudden gush, saturating the whole of his trousers and stomach and pooling around his feet, and it was making a splashing sound on the cobbles, and somewhere he was aware of the patter of tiny feet quickly dashing away, and a tinkling sound as something small dropped onto the ground close to him.

Oliver's legs buckled and turned to jelly, and he seemed to deflate like a balloon as he sank slowly to a squatting position, with his back to the metal wall of the urinal and his feet sticking out. His forehead broke out in a cold but clammy sweat, and he weakly groped at the front of his saddened trousers, his brain fluttering in a sudden panic at the wet stickiness he felt through the torn and ripped material.

The last thing that passed through his mind before he lost consciousness wasn't thoughts of his wife and little baby waiting for him back in London. No, what flashed through his dying brain was the simple question: where have my balls gone?

SCHLOSS HULCHRATH – HITLER YOUTH TRAINING CAMP.
LATE SUMMER 1944

The sound of gunfire broke the still early morning air, the noise echoing across the castle grounds and the small town beyond.

Herbert Wenzel stood in the shade below the beech tree, the low overhanging branches offering shelter from the warm sun. Even though the day was still young, it promised to be another long and hot one as the summer dragged on. There was a faint smell of cooking wafting across from the kitchens as breakfast was prepared, but before they ate he had insisted on the boys turning out for another training session.

There were around about twenty recruits here, lodging at the castle and learning new skills, each one chosen on merit after showing considerable ability and aptitude and energy, a desire to advance their training beyond that of their friends and peers back home. So without their parent's consent they had been brought here to this special facility, to be drilled and instructed and taught like real soldiers, instead of doing simple map-reading and rambling.

As their senior training officer Wenzel realized how important it was to instil in them the necessary discipline required to transform them from mere boy scouts into real fighters. He also understood that with the war going from bad to worse, now that the allied forces were already entrenched in mainland Europe and advancing steadily east towards Germany's borders, that time was of the essence. So every day he and the other instructors pushed them hard, from sunrise until sunset, teaching them such things as first aid, infiltration exercises, close-weapons training, physical conditioning (which included not only increasing their stamina but also character-building sessions of boxing and wrestling), fencing to test their reflexes, hunting and foraging and building shelters in the woods. And also rifle practice like today.

It wasn't strictly necessary for him to be in attendance in person at the daily drills, for the other instructors, dressed in shorts and grey gymnastic vests, were more than capable of instructing the boys adequately. He also felt slightly out of place in full uniform, something which he knew unsettled the recruits and gave them the jitters. But he liked to watch and appraise them, to spot those with promising potential. Boys like Erich Morgenschweiss, the sixteen year-old from Munich. Tall and blond, with a magnificent physique even at his young age, fully committed to the fatherland and their *Fuhrer*, a model Aryan and already a fine soldier. A perfect candidate for the next level of training.

Wenzel watched him closely, impressed with his skill with the rifle. Lying flat on the wooden platform, with the barrel of his gun resting across the sandbag to steady the weapon, he fired shot after shot down the rifle range, hitting the human-shaped target with unerring accuracy.

Very good, very good.

Wenzel made a mental note to take a look at the boy's file later with the intention of putting his name forward and recommending him for the 'special commando unit' that was been discussed back at headquarters in Braunschweig.

In stark contrast was the recruit lying next to him. Short and tubby, with a ruddy face covered in acne, he was a walking disaster when it came to the military training or physical exercise. He was only here because of the boy's family connections, their patronage and donations to the Nazi party over the years allowing him opportunities that would otherwise, certainly on ability, be denied him.

However, the boy was said to be academically very bright, and there were numerous other ways in which he could contribute to the national cause, if only in clerical work or perhaps as an *aide de camp.*

Wenzel went across to where the boy lay, pointing the barrel of the rifle he held in the general direction of the target and squinting at the sights. As he approached the boy fired, the kick from the .22RL thumping back into his shoulder and making him wince. The shot, as usual, went wide, kicking up dust in the pile of soil behind the line of wooden targets.

"No, no," Wenzel implored. "Do not fire when you breathe in. First you exhale, then hold your breath, and gently squeeze the trigger."

There were several sniggers from some of the other recruits, and the boy squirmed in embarrassment. Wenzel looked around for the nearest instructor and beckoned him across.

"Sepp," he addressed him by his nickname, "take this boy off the guns for now. He may be better suited for other duties." He looked down at the boy, not wanting to be too harsh on him. "Do not fret my lad, we will make a soldier out of you yet." He gave him a wink, which seemed to cheer him up.

Just then a junior clerk from the officer's quarters came trotting across the field from the direction of the large round castle tower beyond the footbridge. He drew to a halt before Wenzel, snapped a crisp salute with his right arm shooting out and his heels clicking together.

Wenzel refrained from returning the salute and simply asked, "what is it?"

"Sir, *Obergruppenfuhrer* Prutzmann wishes to see you immediately In his rooms."

Wenzel sighed and took a last look at the recruits, watching as the sixteen-year old Erich Morgenschweiss scored another bullseye, and then turned and followed him.

Schloss Hulchrath wasn't a particularly big or majestic castle compared to those in the Harz Mountains or along the Rhine. It consisted mostly of one large, squat and circular tower which leaned out over the moat like a fat drunk, plus the great hall which stretched back and connected it to several smaller towers and the gatehouse. A number of separate and more modern buildings dating from the 18th Century were clustered together near a long drive that led up from the village, and these had been turned into stables for the officers' horses and sheds for the vehicles. The moat was also a bit of a disappointment, Wenzel thought, for it only curved around a part of the castle in a crescent-moon shape – he presumed that over the centuries parts of it had been filled in and grassed over. The inside was also quite spartan: the rooms were large and bare and with little in the way of medieval refinery or tapestries and so on, they were in fact quite drab, and the boys' dormitory was simple and functional with lines of wooden beds up against both side walls, the room chilled at night by cold draughts blowing through the ancient stonework. But the castle had not been chosen for its beauty or setting, and he doubted if any princes or nobles had ever held it as their seat of power in the region. It was actually a little-known castle tucked away in the back-of-beyond, and as such was perfect for its current purpose as a military training camp for the Hitler-Jugend, the Hitler Youth.

Wenzel followed the clerk along the path and across the narrow footbridge over the moat. As they walked he glanced up towards the wooden hoarding attached to the side of the main tower, for a movement there had caught his eye. This small timber structure, not much more than a covered balcony, would have been used to allow enfilading fire from archers and crossbowmen if the castle had ever come under attack. Although he'd never stepped inside – as access was via Prutzmann's office – Wenzel knew there were gaps in the wooden floor allowing defenders to drop missiles on attackers at the foot of the tower, such as hot water or red-hot sand, or heavy rocks.

Now, however, he was more interested in what had made him look up, for he was sure he had spotted a slim silhouette standing there, almost hidden within the shadows of the structure. Someone looking down at him through the openings of the balcony.

He stared hard, unsure, for the figure now appeared to have stepped back out of sight.

Then he passed beneath the stone roof of the castle's gateway, and it slipped from his view.

Obergruppenfuhrer Hans-Adolf Prutzmann's official title was General Inspector of Special Defence, a promotion sanctioned by *Reichsfuhrer* Heinrich Himmler himself just a month or so ago. Since this appointment his priority had been to set up the training schools both here at Schloss Hulchrath and also at the larger site over in Braunschweig, as well as liaising with Berlin. With these tasks complete he had chosen to base himself here, choosing the rooms on the top floor of the main tower as his private quarters and office.

Wenzel was escorted inside and the door was gently shut behind him, leaving him alone with Prutzmann. Standing before the wide oak desk he waited whilst his superior leaned forward, continuing to read a file spread out before him without once looking up. Wenzel watched the man patiently, seeing his own dim reflection in Prutzmann's highly polished, balding head.

After a minute or so he finally mumbled "sit please," and as Wenzel took the only other seat in the room, Prutzmann closed the file and looked up. His thin lips twitched briefly into what might pass as a smile, before his features slipped back into a neutral expression.

"Is the training going well Wenzel?" Prutzmann's voice was low and gravely, almost a rumble like distant thunder.

"Yes mine *Obergruppenfuhrer*. The recruits are showing impressive potential. The selection process was time-consuming, but as is becoming apparent is proving fully worthwhile. They are mostly ahead of schedule, both in their military disciplines as well as their academic studies."

As he spoke Wenzel cast his eyes around the office, noting the large painting of Alexander the Great above the empty fireplace, the portrait of *The Fuhrer* which hung beside the deep-set window, and the small door in the corner which he knew led out onto the wooden balcony.

"Everything is proceeding exactly as we had hoped," he added with not a small degree of self-satisfaction.

"Excellent," Prutzmann replied. He looked straight at Wenzel with his eyes narrowed in consideration. "Because we have just received final confirmation from the *Reichsfuhrer* that we are to press ahead with the special program."

Wenzel's attention came fully back to the meeting at these words. He found himself subconsciously sitting up in his chair a fraction, and for some unaccountable reason felt a queer prickling sensation at the back of his neck.

Prutzmann gently patted the file on the desk before him. "Here are our final instructions, as obtained and modified during the Magus Conference."

Wenzel's eyes lowered to look at the leather bound file, noticing the strange symbols across the front.

"It is imperative that we follow all of the observances correctly," Prutzmann continued, his hand still touching the file in an almost protective manner. He waited for a response, and so Wenzel merely nodded, for his mouth was suddenly very dry.

Finally Prutzmann took hold of the heavy file and leaned across his desk, holding it out. Wenzel gripped the leather in both his arms as he sat back in his chair, looking down at the cover. On the front, in simple typed words – **UNTERNEHMEN WERWOLF**.

"You may read it tonight and only tonight. The lunar phase is correct. It goes without saying, however, that you should still conduct all of the necessary protective measures."

"Of course *Obergruppenfuhrer*," he managed to reply.

There were several moments of silence between the two men as each thought about what was to come, before Prutzmann quite quickly came to his feet. "Now, I wish you to meet someone."

Wenzel jumped up, making sure not to drop the large file, his eyes automatically shifting over to the small door in the far corner and thinking of the figure he had seen from outside.

As he guessed he would Prutzmann called across in that direction, his voice suddenly more animated. "You may join us please."

The door was pushed open from the other side and in walked a short and young person.

"This is Fraulein Ilse Hirsch," Prutzmann announced.

Wenzel stared in shock and surprise.

Before him stood a strikingly beautiful young woman, he guessed aged in her very early twenties. Quite short and petite with long blonde hair perfectly arranged in a pair of plaits that hung down over the front of her shoulders, and with crystal blue eyes that held his gaze with confidence. She was dressed in the uniform of the BDM, The League of German Girls, the female branch of the Hitler Youth: long dark blue skirt and brown brogues and white socks, and a pristine white short-sleeved blouse and black necktie. Wenzel noticed on her left sleeve the black and silver insignia that gave her rank as Captain, above the small diamond patch with a swastika at the centre.

Wenzel cast his gaze over her, rooted to the spot, and when he glanced back up to her face her ice-cold eyes were now looking not at him but at the file he still gripped tightly to his chest. There was the faintest hint of a smile and her lips parted just a fraction.

Prutzmann, standing to the side, watched them both curiously with his head tilted slightly. Then he blinked lazily and moved around his desk to join them in the centre of the room.

"Fraulein Hirsch has just arrived from Berlin where she has been attending the conference. She kindly brought the file with her."

Wenzel finally dragged his gaze from her and looked across at Prutzmann with his brow furrowed in confusion.

"Do not worry, we may converse freely. Miss Hirsch has code blue clearance and has full access to all special program operations. She is here as our new team member."

"But... but I..." Wenzel stammered, but did not get any further as Prutzmann laughed gently.

"Now, now, do not be surprised. The women of the Third Reich have a very important role to play, and Miss Hirsch has a very special set of skills that will prove vital to us in the weeks ahead. Actually that is the main purpose of her visit. To pass on her incredible knowledge, is it not, Miss Hirsch?"

The young lady, who had so far not spoken a word or barely moved an inch, looked across at Prutzmann and gave the merest nod of her head. Then she turned to once more look straight at Wenzel.

"And in return, under your personal guidance Wenzel, you are to train her as a special defence operative in Commando Unit No 1. I also want you to handpick a squad for immediate field deployment, no more than 4 or 5 people in total. They are to be held in constant readiness for our deep-penetration Swift Strike II Plan."

Wenzel's thoughts were all over the place, his head spinning with all kinds of concerns and questions, but he just couldn't seem to get them in order or to articulate them. He was actually starting to feel a bit of a fool, and he tried desperately to regain his composure.

"Your role as senior training officer makes you ideal for the task," Prutzmann continued. "Assuming you think you are capable and up to it?"

"Of course," Wenzel replied briskly.

Prutzmann nodded slowly. "Just as I thought. Make sure you don't let me down. Things are moving forward with urgent alacrity." Turning to the woman standing beside them he said to her in a gentler voice, "I leave you in Officer Wenzel's capable hands, Miss Hirsch."

Ilse Hirsch, captain of the BDM, replied with the crispest Hitler salute that Wenzel thought he had ever seen. With her eyes fixed on him, her lips once more parted in the merest of smiles, revealing a row of sharp little teeth.

Making his skin crawl and his heart shiver.

*   *   *

4 WEEKS LATER

The four of them moved through the woods in single-file, treading carefully on the brown leaves and small twigs that carpeted the floor. Although only an exercise, and even though they were still deep inside friendly territory, they desired to make as little noise as possible lest any prying eyes or ears noticed them.

Dressed in heavy dark green coveralls and fur-lined overcoats to keep the autumnal chill away, together with strong military boots and knapsacks, they walked steadily on, glancing around at the trees and undergrowth in continuous alert to their surroundings. The sky was steadily darkening, even more so beneath the canopy of branches overhead, and each of them looked forward to a warm camp fire and hot food in their stomachs.

At the front, leading the little band, Fraulein Hirsch came to a sudden stop.

"This will do," she told the others.

Wenzel, who was just behind her, moved cautiously forward to peer over her shoulder to see where she was pointing. Out of the corner of his eye he also glanced at her profile, unable to stop himself.

Since that first meeting back in Prutzmann's office, the two of them had spent every single day working together. From his initial feeling of unease, he had developed a certain amount of respect for her. Far from been a hindrance and an extra responsibility to add to all of the others, he'd actually soon learned that she was a very capable and well-trained operative, much more so than most other girls in the BDM, who he knew spent most of their time either playing sports or training as their roles as women in German society, as wife, mother and homemaker.

But Ilse Hirsch was already a highly skilled female soldier, an expert marksman and very adept at most other commando techniques, whether it was climbing an enemy watchtower and

41

quickly dispatching an enemy lookout with a garrotte, or making a homemade bomb from a tin of Heinz soup so loved by the American GI's. In actual fact, as Prutzmann had indicated, she also had other skills: her knowledge of bush craft for example was first-class, better than his own he had to admit, and over the last week or so whilst they had been conducting their training in the woods east of Schloss Hulchrath, she had taught many of these survival skills to himself and the others in their party.

He was also, in truth, in awe of her beauty. Ice-cold though her personality could be, he actually found this immensely attractive and alluring. She had an animal magnetism about her that grabbed him in its claws like some helpless prey. A little bit, he mused, like the animals that they were setting snares for right now.

"Just ahead there. You can see the trail and spoors just outside the opening in the ground." She slung off her knapsack and started to rummage inside. "If we set the snare just outside, the rabbit will run straight into the wire loop. While we do that, the other two can set up another sapling trap over in that copse like I showed them earlier."

The other two members of the team, instructor Leitgeb who everybody called 'Sepp' for some reason, and the young teenager Erich Morgenschweiss, both looked to where she indicated, nodded eagerly and strolled off. As they moved through the trees, young Erich couldn't resist glancing back over his shoulder at her, something that Hirsch herself noticed.

Wenzel watched as she set the snare before the rabbit den. He passed her some bait which she placed just the far side of the wire loop. As she worked she looked over towards the others, who were bending a slim branch of one of the saplings down to the ground before attaching a snare from the branch to the small wooden stake they had placed in the ground. "They need to make the trigger-action more precise, so that the slightest movement sets it off." She shook her head as she spoke. "Also, if the branch snaps up too high it will pull the head right off the creature like last time. Once it bleeds into the carcass it becomes inedible. Unless you like to eat your meat raw," she joked, with a sly smile at Wenzel.

He grinned back. "I don't think their stomachs would cope, especially the young boy. He might pretend to be tough, but he is a city boy and used to hearty home-cooked food."

Hirsch listened, her eyes flicking back to the youngest of their little group. She wiped her forehead with her hand, leaving a smear of dirt on her skin. "He wants to fuck me," she told him simply.

Wenzel was thrown for a moment, not used to bawdy bar-room language from a woman.

"But most men do, so it will not be a problem. Our training is our priority, and our mission to come. There can be no distractions." She stood up, her body so close to him that it brushed slightly against his. "If it starts to be a difficulty, I will let him. And then we continue as before."

Hirsch turned to move away, and Wenzel licked his lips which were suddenly as dry as sandpaper.

She turned back again. "Tonight, I share your dugout Wenzel." Then she marched off through the trees.

They reached their campsite about one hour later, after they had set their snares and one more deadfall trap, hoping to eat rabbit or squirrel in the morning. For their evening meal they would have to make do with canned meat heated above a fire, and some biscuits.

They had chosen a site on the south-facing side of a heavily wooded slope, close to where a small brook flowed. It consisted of three underground dugouts, two for sleeping two people each, and the third to stockpile supplies of food and weapons. Similar arms caches were placed throughout the local countryside, their location marked on their map which they would hand in once they returned to Hulchrath.

The dugouts were constructed so as not to destroy the trees around them and thus give away their location. Once closed for the night or for longer periods, they would be virtually impossible to spot from above ground, their wooden entrances covered as they were with undergrowth and leaf-mould to camouflage them. The way in and out was an opening about two feet across which went straight down several feet before opening out into a horizontal space roughly 8 to 10 feet long and wide enough for two people to sleep and move about in reasonable comfort. Each had a wooden floor plus a drainage ditch on the downward side, and the walls and roof were reinforced with timber, making them snug and mostly soundproof.

They ate their supper quietly, sharing a few words in hushed tones. Wenzel sat across the small fire from his two male colleagues, while Hirsch boiled up a small Gerry can of water to make coffee. Once it was done she handed it around. He noticed Morgenschweiss still darting the odd glimpse at her when he thought she wasn't looking, but the small exchange of glances she shared with Wenzel told him she was fully aware of the boy's interest. This perturbed him. In spite of her earlier insistence that she would not allow this to become an issue, Wenzel could foresee problems ahead. It was something he would need to keep an eye on, and if necessary make it clear to the boy why it might potentially be required to drop him from the unit.

After a short time Wenzel decided it was time to turn in. They had one more day to go with the usual dawn start, and then they were to make their way back. The other two shuffled off. Hirsch poured water onto the fire and kicked and smoothed away any traces, then covered it over with leaves. She followed him over to their dugout, squirmed down into the entrance, and Wenzel follow suit.

The inside was already lit with a small oil lamp. They both settled down in their positions side by side, their bodies pushed up against each other, and without any words closed their eyes and waited for sleep.

Somewhere outside, in the distance, Wenzel heard the distinctive howl of a wolf. The sound made his skin crawl, but when he looked over at Hirsch he saw her eyes wide and glistening in the light from the lamp, a sheen of perspiration on her upper lip. He closed his eyes once more and tried to sleep.

"Damn it," Hirsch suddenly said. Wenzel turned to gaze at her once again, to see she was sitting up and already looking at him. She stared long and hard, her brow furrowed in thought. Then, to his amazement, she commenced to undress, removing her coverall and kicking it down towards the end of the dugout. And she removed her underclothes, Wenzel seeing her hard nipples and her blonde plaits coiled down over her stomach, and the pink flush between her legs which she opened wide for him.

Eyes burning into him like icy diamonds.

"Come," she told him.

*   *   *

They made it back to Schloss Hulchrath on time the following evening, the castle and grounds mostly in darkness except for a few lights burning in the highest windows. Sepp and the boy made straight for the kitchens where a hot meal awaited them, but Wenzel and Fraulein Hirsch were both summoned to *Obergruppenfuhrer* Prutzmann's office on the top floor.

As they ascended the narrow staircase Wenzel reflected again on last night's events. The animal ferocity of their coupling – Wenzel would not describe it as love-making, for it was quick and wild and savage – had left him physically spent and mentally confused. Once they were both finished, she had pushed him away, telling him simply to sleep, and no further words were exchanged on the subject, not last night or this morning. Hirsch had simply carried on as though nothing had happened. But throughout the day Wenzel had pondered on things, his mind trying to fathom this strange woman, but unable to reach any conclusions. She was a total enigma to him. He had also begun to wonder what exactly was the real purpose for her being sent to Hulchrath? What role was she to play? The fact that she had attended the mysterious Magus Conference with the hierarchy of Nazi Germany told him she was not simply here to learn commando training.

Prutzmann was waiting for them in his office. As they went through their debrief, Wenzel sensed a certain agitation from his superior, the way he fidgeted and shuffled about. Eventually, he raised his hand to interrupt them.

"Yes, I'm sure everything went well. Perhaps we can skip the details tonight, I will read your full report when you present it in the morning."

Then he clasped his hands together and smiled broadly, the most animated that Wenzel had ever seen him. He and Hirsch exchanged a glance.

Reaching out, he pulled out a slip of paper from his desk drawer, and fluttered it in the air before them. "Another communiqué from Berlin," he explained.

Wenzel and Hirsch waited.

"Our blue-print for Swift Strike II has been sanctioned." He rocked back and forward, his shoulders shivering in barely-suppressed excitement. "Unternehmen Werwolf!"

Unternehmen Werwolf, Wenzel thought.

Operation Werewolf.

CHAPTER 5

WORKING THE CASE

The location of the body – still inside the urinal – made it impossible to cover it over with a white forensic tent, and so a number of dark boards and sheets had been erected around the spot, both on the pathway and the canal side, blocking the view of the ghouls and gawkers.

Pieter made his way across the cobbles of Oudekerksplein, which were wet and glistening, not from early morning rain but from the road sweeper which was making its slow way around the square. He noted the time on his mobile – 06:42am. Approx. thirty minutes since he'd received the call, and nearly ninety minutes since the body was found. As he watched the cleaners go about their task he could almost visualise them cleaning and scrubbing away any forensic evidence right before his eyes, and he shook his head, not for the first time bewildered by the incompetence of the Amsterdam Police Department.

Across the other side of the canal, on the corner where the bridge was, he saw Daan Beumers standing and talking with a young couple, and he raised a weary wave which his colleague returned. Then, after showing his pass, Pieter ducked through the narrow gap in the wooden boards and entered the crime scene.

A pair of forensic techs were working around the periphery of the urinal. They may have been the same two from the murder two nights ago, but clad in their white get-up and with hoods and masks covering their faces, they had the appearance of NASA astronauts, and so it was impossible to tell. At the moment they were busy using what looked like a tiny hand-held mini-vacuum, sucking up microscopic detritus from the ground. To the side was a large silver crate which was opened out a little like a fishing-tackle box, filled with vials and brushes and fancy gizmos.

The body was still in-situ, as of yet not disturbed apart from two plastic bags covering the deceased's fingernails.

Pieter stepped forward to take a closer look.

The male victim was crammed unceremoniously inside the urinal, all crumpled up and folded into the cramped space near the ground. One of his legs was folded underneath him, the other one sticking straight out into the open, so that he was squatting just above the small drain cover that people pissed into. Pieter immediately saw the dark, damp patch around the man's crotch area, and the ripped trousers there, as well as the huge loss of blood from what was quite obviously a large stab wound in that part of his anatomy. Much of the blood from the ugly-looking rent would have splashed straight into the drain and been lost forever, but there was still a large pool of it staining the cobbles. The victim's hands hung loose at his sides, and his head lolled back to rest against the back of the metal urinal, the face already starting to turn a blackish colour from the first signs of decomposition.

Pieter moved sideways around the urinal, intending to pass around the back and look down into the canal itself, his mind already thinking about where any murder weapon might have been disposed. But the boards there went right up the edge of the canal, stopping his circumnavigation, and anyway he didn't much fancy risking an early morning dip. Coming back round he took note of the forensic guys scowling at him, no doubt fretting over their precious crime-scene, and so taking the hint Pieter squeezed back through the opening and made his way across the bridge.

As he approached, Daan Beumers was still speaking to the couple, but on seeing Pieter heading his way he broke off from their conversation. The man and woman waited patiently.

"Morning boss."

He was wearing a bright white tracksuit with matching plimsolls, sticking out like a sore thumb. He looked very self-conscious.

"What's with the gear? I never had you down as an early-morning jogger."

"Ah, this? The girlfriend bought it for me last Christmas. She's currently on another health push, which means by default that I'm also on another health push, and so some mornings I wear it when I leave for work to let her think I'm taking it seriously. I normally park up around the corner and change clothes, but I never got the chance this morning before I got called over here."

"Looks expensive," Pieter nodded at the fancy running shoes.

"You're telling me."

"Give me the run-down then."

Beumers leaned on the bridge railing, the early-morning sun behind his back casting his shadow on the water below. "The body was spotted just after five this morning by those street cleaners. They were doing their usual rounds when one of them, an enterprising young guy who is new on the job, decided to jet wash inside the urinal. Probably the first time in years that it's been done, those places stink something terrible. Anyway, he spotted the guy just before he turned on his thingamebob, thought he was either a crackhead or someone sleeping off too many tequilas, until he noticed the guy's pecker sticking out of his pants was all mangled up. He raised the alarm, or rather his boss in the road sweeper did when he saw the kid crawling on his hands and knees puking up his syrup pancakes. Our guys were here within a few minutes, but in the meantime Mr Jobsworth, in his nice warm cabin there, went straight back to work cleaning the square. Fucking fucktard, has he never seen CSI Miami? Says he has a schedule to keep."

"Just the single injury?"

"From the looks of it yes. Sliced his balls clean off. Luckily they were too big to disappear down into the drain, so at least they can be reattached by the undertaker in time for the viewing. He had a few scratches and bruises here and there but they were probably self-inflicted whilst he'd be no doubt thrashing about."

Pieter looked over to where the urinal was, surrounded by the boards and sheets. A black van with blacked-out windows was just pulling up alongside.

"Please tell me we have ID'd him this time?"

"Oh yeah, pretty straight forward compared to the other night. He had credit cards on him – which obviously rules out robbery – as well as a hotel key-card for the Ibis next to Centraal Station. Dead guy is a Mr Oliver Monroe, from London."

"A tourist, or here on business?"

Beumers shrugged. "He was booked in for just one night, so he could be either. We have a phone number for his home address, but given the early time we haven't made the call yet. Might as well let his family have another few hours of blessed ignorance in bed before we shatter their lives."

Pieter turned and nodded to the young couple still waiting at the end of the bridge.

Beumers followed his gaze. "We have witnesses boss."

"They saw the murder?" Pieter asked hopefully, before his colleague shook his head.

"Not the actual killing, no. But they might have seen the killers."

"Killers? As in plural?"

"Yep."

Beumers led him over to where the man and woman stood hugging each other either from shock or because of the chilly morning air.

They turned out to be a young couple staying in a backpacker's hostel over on Zeedijk. They were rocking the 70's look, her wearing a vintage sleeveless sheepskin jacket and he a pair of bright yellow cord trousers probably bought at the market at Waterloosplein. Their names were Henrietta and Maarten. After brief introductions, Daan Beumers asked them to repeat what they had been telling him.

"We'd been over in Grasshoppers sampling the menu, and we decided to head back to our room, and so cut through here to cross the bridge," the guy explained. "We are celebrating the first anniversary of our non-commitment binary relationship."

Pieter smiled what he hoped passed as a warm smile.

"Anyway we stopped to take a photograph right at this spot. And that's when we saw the commotion over there."

"It was so strange," Henrietta picked up the story. "No screaming or shouting, just lots of running with figures dashing about, like a scuffle or a mugging or something."

"Over at the public urinal?" Pieter enquired.

"Yes," Maarten confirmed. "Even though it was late, this area is always well lit, and we could tell something bad was happening."

"And then we saw them. Three people running right past us, over the bridge and down the alley behind us, heading towards the next canal. They literally passed within about three feet of where we are standing."

Pieter looked around, noticing that there were no obvious security cameras covering the route, but there was a café right on the corner there which might have its own CCTV coverage.

"Did you get a good look at them?" he asked.

"Not really. They were wearing black coats with their hoods turned up, and we were kinda stepping back to get out of their way." Henrietta gave an exaggerated shiver, and Maarten hugged her tightly, his hand slipping down to gently squeeze her bum. "It was a bit of a shock, you know? Especially because of their age."

Pieter caught the sideways glance that Beumers gave him – this part was apparently new to him. "How so?" A weird feeling made his tummy give a peculiar backflip.

"Well, one of them was an adult. Quite slim but definitely an adult. But the other two, the ones at the back, they were just kids. Small, but not too young, I'd say teenage lads."

Pieter walked to the side of the bridge and stood by the railing. After a moment he turned, and leaned on it. "You're sure? Absolutely sure about that?"

Henrietta and Maarten both nodded.

"And what time was this, approximately?"

"2:07am" Maarten responded without missing a beat.

Pieter felt his eyebrows shoot up like Groucho Marx's.

Maarten fished into his trouser pocket and brought out his mobile, tapped on the screen and showed him the picture that they had been taking at the time, him and her playing tonsil tennis, the photo apparently done with a selfie-stick. He then went into the properties menu which showed the exact date and time, which was exactly as he'd said.

"When we heard from a friend at the hostel about a murder, right over there at the toilet, then we thought we should come and talk to the police. But you know what the strangest thing of all was?"

Pieter waited, not sure if he wanted to hear or not.

"They moved so fast. Literally in a blur. They were gone by us like that," he clicked his fingers for effect. "Oh I know teenagers can move, but this was ridiculously fast. We stepped out of their way, as I say, but I twisted around to shout after them, but in the half second it took they were gone. Right the way down the end of that alleyway, which is quite long and straight, and then puff, they had vanished. Like those street magicians."

After taking their details they thanked the couple and strolled back across the small bridge.

"What do you make of that then?" Pieter asked the police sergeant

"About them moving so fast? Or the ages of the suspects?

"Both."

"Well more likely the guy was more shaken than he says and just took longer to gather his wits and react, so they were away and around the far corner before he knew what's what. As for them being teenagers, nothing surprises me in this city anymore, so I guess it's feasible. Either that or we have a gang of homicidal dwarfs roaming the streets."

Pieter shoved his hands deep into his coat pockets as he turned things over in his mind.

"But at least we have an exact time for the murder," Beumers added optimistically. "Assuming they saw what they saw." He glanced at his superior as they walked. "Are we linking this one with the other boss? Officially?"

"Only semi-officially for now. Going off the victims, a prostitute and someone having a night of fun in the red light district, I'd say that it's a strong likelihood that they are linked."

"Like vigilantes? Someone cleaning up the area? Doing what the city council have been promising to do for years now? I fucking hope not, what a clusterfuck that can of worms could turn out to be. I hate fucking politics."

As they stepped down off the bridge and cut across the corner to head back to the hive of activity around the urinal, Pieter saw one of the forensic techies push through the small cluster of onlookers that had started to gather, commuters on their way to work. The white-clad spaceman fairly bounced across to them, evidently excited about something. He thrust out a clear-plastic evidence bag, waggling it right in Pieter's face.

"We've found something. On the ground just outside the pisser."

Pieter took the bag and peered at the tiny object inside.

"It's a miracle the street cleaner didn't suck it up, otherwise we'd never have been any the wiser."

Inside was a small silver signet ring. Around the edge of the ring was some writing, in fancy script. On the front a skull and crossbones above the letter W.

Pieter decided to take the small evidence bag back to HQ as he had a hunch on who might be able to offer some help regarding the signet ring. In the meantime he asked Beumers to get the owner of the small corner café to open up and show him their camera footage, if they had any.

Daan Beumers was in luck on two counts. The café owner, Mr Saleem, was all too keen to help as he had a young cousin who was due to pass out at the police training academy over in Eindhoven in a few weeks. And yes, they did have security cameras which filmed 24hrs per day, one of which covered the street and bridge outside. Perfect!

Mr Saleem showed him how to fast-forward or pause the footage on his small laptop in a backroom, and then left him alone to get ready for the lunchtime trade in a few hours. Leaning forward over the monitor Daan raced through the early stuff which showed the usual evening revellers, until he reached the timeframe in question. He watched from shortly before 2am just on the off chance that the camera may have caught the suspects before the murder, but alas nothing of interest stood out. But as the clock in the top right corner clicked over to 2.05am he saw quite clearly in the sharp black and white footage the young couple, Henrietta and Maarten, hove into view as they crossed the bridge from the Oude Kerk side. He watched them stroll across hand-in-hand and then saunter to the bridge handrail, where Maarten fished out his extendable selfie-stick from somewhere and lifted it and the attached mobile high into the air, snapping a pic as the lovebirds smooched and cuddled.

Both of them turned to glance at something, which was annoyingly off camera, and then suddenly stumble quickly away in alarm. And in the next instant, there was a dark blur, more of a smudge on the camera, as some shadow or whatever raced by them in a flash.

Daan sat up rigidly in the chair. "What the fuck?"

For several seconds he didn't move, just stared open-mouthed at the screen, which now showed the young couple staring at something, again off camera, with similar expressions of shock on their faces.

Snapping out of his paralysis, Daan quickly paused the footage, then ran it back to watch the sequence again. And once more watched the bizarre shadow – for that's what it appeared to be – race by at ridiculous speed. Exactly as they had described.

Again he ran it back. But this time he tried to pause it at the split-second that the blurry thing was on screen, toddling the film back and forth until he had the best shot possible. Then Daan sat back in his chair and stared at what was on the screen in front of him.

It was the unmistakable figure of a child, but dressed in either a black coat or a fucking weird-looking hooded cloak. And within the hood, too indistinct and out of focus to see much, was a pale face. And where the mouth should be a horrible black maw, below a pair of deep shadowy eye sockets.

Floris de Kok worked in the basement level at Police HQ. He was a civilian worker, but unlike his colleagues who worked in the large office pool on the ground floor, he preferred the peace and quiet down here. The privacy also meant he could avoid the curious stares and intrusive questions that his embarrassing ailment provoked.

Floris suffered from essential tremor, a disorder that caused involuntary shaking of his hands, something that had troubled him since first developing the problem when he was in his late thirties, about ten years ago. Despite what people presumed, it was *not* connected to Parkinson's disease in any way, nor was it a result of excess drinking. But after a while the blatant stares and ignorant comments had ground him down so much that one day last year, totally cheesed off, Floris had uprooted from his desk upstairs and moved shop down to the small room just along the corridor from the underground car pool. And here he stayed, from 8 till 5, not even leaving for lunch, scanning documents and filing away forms and tagging up evidence.

Floris was also a bit of a history buff, especially military history. At weekends he sometimes took part in Napoleonic battle re-enactments with fellow enthusiasts, but his interest covered all periods of conflict, down to the tiniest detail.

Because of this, and the tremors, he had been given the unfortunate nickname of Adolf. Even though he looked nothing like the genocidal madman, Floris with his long hair and tattoos and no moustache. Hiding away underground probably didn't help matters. So the name stuck, and Floris didn't really mind.

When he heard the footsteps coming down the stairs he hoped it was just another cop come to sign out a vehicle from the parking lot, but when they paused outside his tiny office he knew someone was calling around for something, and he sighed in annoyance. When the door opened, however, and Pieter Van Dijk walked in Floris broke off from what he was doing, glad for the interruption. Pieter was ok.

"Hey buddy," he greeted his visitor.

"Adolf, my man, how's it hanging?" Pieter grabbed the room's spare seat, and sat down, before whizzing across on its wheels until he was alongside Floris' desk.

"Oh you know, topping up my vitamin D." He closed the lid on the large file box, wrote something on the top, and added it to the pile on the floor. He noticed the small evidence bag that Pieter was holding. "What can I do for you?"

Pieter tossed the clear plastic bag onto the desk, its contents chinking quietly. "Can you identify this at all? Or at least tell me something about it?"

Floris picked it up and peered at the silver ring inside, turning it this way and that.

"Something about the emblem on the front rang a few bells," Pieter added. He pointed at the tiny skull and cross bones with his little finger. "I'm thinking World War 2, perhaps the SS? Or am I way off the mark?"

"Fascinating," Floris murmured, his eyes glinting with excitement.

Pieter waited while Floris studied the item, noticing a tremor starting up in his friend's arm but saying nothing.

"You're almost right. Certainly WW2, and Nazi-era. But the skull and crossbones are a little different from the *Totenkopf* – that's the SS Death's Head Symbol that the officers wore on their peaked caps. And the large W underneath doesn't stand for the *Wehrmacht* – that's what the German Army was called back then," he informed him.

"So it stands for…what?"

Floris didn't reply to the question, instead he peered at the writing etched into the side of the ring. "This here looks like some very old Nordic script, Norse as it was called hundreds of years ago. Yes, very fascinating." He peered up over the top of the evidence bag at Pieter. "I could find out for you, but it might take a day or two. There's a lot of stuff on the internet about this, but I have tonnes of books back home all about the rise of the Nazis, the Third Reich and so on, with some excellent illustrations of German uniforms and regalia. I could go through them for you if you like?"

"That would be cool."

"I don't suppose I'm allowed to take this home with me?" He hefted the plastic bag and the ring.

"Afraid not. But you can take as many photos as you like." Pieter put on a pair of plastic gloves and then spread out another brand new evidence bag across the desk, took out the ring very carefully and laid it on the surface.

When Floris was done taking pictures with his mobile Pieter bagged it back up and headed back out the door.

"See you later Adolf."

When he returned to his office on the top floor he pulled out his own mobile and saw that he had a message from Daan Beumers. Apparently there was something odd on the CCTV from the café, and so he was following it up, calling around at various premises along the alley where the three suspects had fled to see if they had security cam footage of their own. No further details. Pieter pocketed the phone.

The autopsy on the dead man from London was due to start around about now but Pieter had no desire or need to be present, and as any conclusions or toxicology reports wouldn't come through until at least tomorrow, he decided to check on how things were progressing with the Mila case.

The first thing to do was to see if any progress had been made with her pimp. He had been brought in for questioning and remanded in custody on human-trafficking charges, so now Pieter turned his attention to his alibi. Going into his Gmail account, Pieter found an email waiting for him.

Cyber cops had been busy. They had checked the pimp's smart TV and fire stick, going through his movie downloads. One of those which he had streamed from Prime – indeed it was La La Land! – was time-stamped as commencing at 9.46pm, which fit into his story time-wise, especially if he had fallen asleep for a while before going to check on his girl and discovering her corpse just before midnight. Additionally forensic guys had done a thorough sweep through his flat and found not a single microscopic drop of blood anywhere. The same with the clothes he had been wearing at the time, all of which had immediately been seized and bagged-up. Considering how blood-splattered Mila's killer would be – "literally dripping in it" as Beumers had put it – it was impossible to escape the conclusion that the pimp may have been telling the truth for possibly the first time in his life.

There was also the inescapable fact that Mila's pimp had been in his cell under lock and key at the time that Oliver Monroe was getting himself murdered, assuming the two deaths were linked of course.

Frustratingly there were still no witnesses coming forward from the other girls working in the window brothels, and also no luck from the CCTV control booth behind Durty Nellies Pub. The people there were not exactly feeling particularly helpful in that regards, and Pieter was just considering whether to apply for a search warrant to allow a more thorough search, when he felt his mobile vibrate in his pocket.

Taking it out he looked at the screen.

It read: **Lotte**

They had an agreement never to bother each other or to have any contact outside of his visits to the Newcastle Bar. Both had preferred it that way, not wanting to become too much a part of each other's lives. It was less hassle and felt better. But they had exchanged numbers fairly early on in their friendship, just in case. And now Lotte was calling him, breaking their little rule.

Something was up.

CHAPTER 6

CONFRONTATIONS AND DREAMS

Pieter didn't put the lights or the siren on as it wasn't that kind of emergency, but the call from Lotte had alarmed him enough to make him drive with a certain aggression through the busy afternoon traffic, weaving around the other cars and bicycles and trams.

It was obvious from the shaky voice and breathy words that she was very upset, and although she tried well to mask the fact, Pieter knew she had been crying. Without elaborating on what was the matter, she made it clear in her trembling voice that she really needed to see him.

Where are you? he had asked.

At the small café in The American Book Centre on Spui Square, she told him.

He'd be there in ten minutes.

Even though part of it was supposed to be for trams only, Pieter went by the most direct route from the Police HQ on Elandsgracht to Spui, heading straight along to Leidseplein and then turning left to zip by the pavement cafes, to pick up the wide thoroughfare of Rokin at the bottom.

It was as he was honking his way through the traffic near the Bulldog Coffeeshop that he caught sight of them both, sitting on a bench side by side, with about half a dozen cans of cheap cider lined up on the pavement before them and a pile of empty ones in the trash can close by. The two of them quite obviously much the worse for wear.

Dad and his boozy lady friend Famke.

Pieter swore out loud, the implications immediately clear to him, and he swerved hard across the path of an oncoming tram, and pulled in at the side of the roadway. From where they were sitting across Leidseplein they would not see him, and anyway they were pretty much too lost in their drunkenness to even notice the world around them, laughing and fooling around.

Pieter moved as if to jump out of the car, but then paused, thinking about Lotte waiting for him. He looked again at his dad, his mind torn, a huge welter of anger and frustration and disappointment filling him. He slammed at the steering wheel, *fuck, fuck, fuck!* And then he sat back in his seat, and shifted the car into automatic, and drove away with his tyres spinning and scrapping against the kerb. He took one final look at them both in his rear view mirror before he lost sight of them amidst the hustle and bustle.

As soon as he arrived, Lotte, who was sitting waiting for him in one of the window seats, jumped to her feet and flung her arms around him, and the sobbing burst forth. She clung to him tightly, her body quivering and shaking against his, and Pieter hugged her back.

After a minute or so he gently steered her back to her seat and he sat on the cushioned wooden bench next to her with his arm still around her shoulder. With her head tilted against his shoulder, Lotte quietly dabbed her tears away.

The café was a small place that he popped into occasionally, and it was never very busy, most times with perhaps just one or two customers sitting quietly in the peaceful atmosphere of the bookshop. The owner – a bit-part TV actress from Spain – waited until Lotte had settled, before she came across and asked politely if she could get them anything. Pieter ordered two cappuccinos. After bringing them over, the owner settled back behind her counter and went back to reading a paperback.

Pieter and Lotte talked for around an hour, during which time the whole sad story slowly and painfully came out.

Lotte was from a non EU nation, and upon deciding she wished to stay and work in Amsterdam she had applied for her GVVA work permit. However, these were only intended for short three month periods, and like so many young people doing casual work for cash, she had neglected to renew it or to apply for a residency visa. It had expired a long time ago, but she had continued working as before without informing her boss at The Newcastle Bar.

Everything had been fine. She enjoyed her job, liked the city, and had a nice rented flat that she had recently re-decorated at her own expense. She was actually starting to think of Amsterdam as her home. But then Bart, her boss, had found out about the expired permit. And instead of reporting her to the city council or terminating her employment, he had instead decided to exploit the situation for himself.

Pieter sat and listened, knowing very well where it was headed, but letting Lotte talk. A slow-burning fuse fizzed and flared inside him. The threats came first, making her work longer and longer shifts. Then the sly touches, Bart squeezing his bulky frame passed her at every opportunity, laughing jokingly if his hand just happened to linger on her waist or glide across her bottom. After a while becoming more blatant whenever the bar was quiet, or perhaps she would be working in the stock room and she would turn to find him behind her, blocking the doorway and leering at her. The groping becoming more intimidating and direct, no longer pretending it was accidental, but just trapping her in the corner and fondling her breasts, pulling her top up or grinding himself against her. Pieter felt sickened as Lotte described how he had forced her to go down on her knees and perform oral sex on him while his hand slipped down her jeans, all the while threatening to inform the authorities if she "misbehaved" or "refused".

With Lotte too terrified or confused not to, her mind filled with thoughts of court-action or ending up in an immigration centre somewhere, she had found herself trapped in this degrading and frightful situation. But after weeks of suffering this horrendous nightmare she had eventually turned for help from the one person who she could trust, even though that person was a police officer.

Pieter shushed her, and put his arm very gently around her shoulder once again, talking to her in a soothing voice – but all the while seething with anger inside. She had done the right thing, he told her. This ends now.

He dropped her off at her flat out near De Gooyer, briefly going inside with her to ensure she was going to be ok before heading off. Lotte wasn't stupid and had a pretty good idea of what he was going to do next, so she implored with him to be careful, not get himself in serious trouble. To his surprise she reached up and put her arms around his neck, pressing her tear-stained cheek against his own cheek, squeezing her fingers into the hair at the back of his head. Promising her he would be back soon, Pieter left.

*   *   *

The bar was quiet at that time of the afternoon – not that it would have made any difference had the place been packed with customers – and so Pieter went barrelling straight in and grabbed a hold of Bart by the back of his jacket, taking him utterly by surprise. Spinning him around in one fluid movement he ran the fat pervert straight through to the toilet, using his head as a battering ram to smash open the door. Kicking it shut behind him, Pieter pushed Bart's face straight into the toilet bowl and flushed it.

After keeping his head under the water for about a minute, Pieter lifted him clear. Bart spluttered and coughed, his face beetroot-red, and he just had time to recognize Pieter before a fist hit him straight in the mouth and split his lip. Pieter hit him in the face again, five or six times, and then slammed his fist as hard as he could into the side of the man's stomach just about where his kidneys would be. Bart slumped across the toilet bowl, badly winded and gasping for breath, his legs like jelly and unable to support his overweight body. Pieter let him slither down onto the dirty floor in between the toilet and the tiny sink,

62

lifted up his foot, and brought his heavy work shoe down onto the back of the head, hearing the satisfying crunch as Bart's nose was mashed into the floor.

Looking at the pile of human waste before him, Pieter gave himself a moment to get his own breath back, his lips drawn back in an ugly grimace. Then he reached down and hauled Bart up, dragging him into a sitting position and twisting the bloodied head about so that their faces were just inches apart.

"Leave her the fuck alone, you fat fuck," he whispered coldly.

Then Pieter left, the few inquisitive customers making way for him.

He went straight back to Lotte's through the evening rush hour, the snarled and congested roads allowing him time to calm down and think things over. As he drove his eyes would occasionally glance down at his hands on the steering wheel, seeing the scuffs and grazes on the knuckles. He realized there was a slim chance that Bart would make an official complaint of assault, and that would filter through to his bosses at HQ and likely result in temporary suspension while the incident was looked at, but he felt fairly sure that the last thing Bart wanted was to involve the police. So on that score Pieter wasn't overly concerned. He could also expedite Lotte's residency application with the Immigration Department, and make sure she scored enough points with the decision-making panel to be granted a Type II Permit – assuming she still wished to stay, which Pieter reckoned might no longer be the case.

He also thought about his dad, his heart sinking at the knowledge that he was once more hitting the booze. As with all alcoholics and people suffering with other addictions, the road to recovery seemed never ending, a pathway beset with problems and setbacks. Pieter just wasn't sure he had the mental reserves to cope with everything that it entailed, as his dad's sponsor and only relative, and all of the responsibilities that came with that.

With these concerns weighing him down – plus the increasingly complex case he was currently leading at work – Pieter parked the car and walked back up the stairs to Lotte's second-floor apartment.

Knocking on the door he waited, hearing faint movement inside, and he looked straight at the tiny security peephole in the door to give Lotte a clear view of his face. A chain was pulled back and then the door opened, her relieved face peering out at him.

They hugged again, and she quickly locked the door. As he followed her though to the small kitchen he saw she had changed into jogging bottoms and a loose jumper. The coffee machine was gurgling away on the counter and she poured him a drink, then leaned back against the wall, sipping from her own cup and hugging it for warmth.

She peered up at him, the faintest of smiles on her lips. He could almost feel the tension sloughing off her.

"So what happened?" she whispered.

Pieter blew air out between his lips, and then shrugged. "Probably best not to go into details too much," he told her. "But he got the message."

Lotte nodded, more to herself if anything. "It's a mess. I was stupid to let things get that bad, I really shouldn't have."

"Hey, there's only one person to blame here, and you and I know who that is."

"I know, but I could have asked you for help sooner. To even let that creep control me like that. I never thought I'd be so...weak...feeble...to allow that."

"He was manipulative, and he thought he had you trapped in an impossible situation. A real nasty piece of work. I come across men like that all of the time, and the one thing they all have in common is this weird ability, almost like an affinity, to home in on the vulnerable and frightened. I'm fairly certain you probably aren't the first woman he has done that kind of thing to."

Lotte listened, and then her brow furrowed as something occurred to her, the alarm making her shudder. "He knows where I live. He's never been here, but he has my address and contact details."

"Hey, don't panic. He'd have to be an absolute moron to come around, and I think even Bart isn't that much of a dimwit. Another thing guys like that have in common is that they don't like confrontation, especially with men. They are cowards essentially."

Lotte looked around nervously, at the doors and windows. She didn't seem very convinced at his reassurances.

Licking her lips, she nodded, and then moved across to a wooden dresser lined with plates and saucers, and reached up for a small delftware pot on the top shelf. Opening the lid she tipped out a key into her hand, and then held it out to him. "This is a spare set, for the front door and also the main door at the bottom of the stairs. Would you have it? Just in case? It'll make me feel a lot better."

Pieter took it and slipped it in his jacket pocket.

"You can use it anytime you like, just to let yourself in and out. Even if I'm not here. I'm sorry for been a complete wuss," she smiled weakly, and Pieter smiled back.

They moved into the main lounge, taking their drinks with them, and sat by the small coffee table. Here they chatted about the situation for a long while, Pieter trying to put her mind at rest, speaking in a gentle voice, and by the time he left the apartment he thought she seemed more positive and reassured.

"Try not to worry," he told her in the doorway. "You've had a horrid ordeal, but I'll deal with everything."

It was early evening by the time he reached his own place, a tall and elegant canal house with a bell gable. The Singel tended to be quiet after dark with most of the nightlife across the far side of Dam Square, and this was the main reason for choosing the area as his home.

The house itself, four stories high, was, like most Amsterdam homes, ridiculously narrow. Each floor was accessed by twisting and rickety wooden staircases, with the rooms small and cramped. Even so, he spent most of his time in the living areas on the top two stories. Here there was the living room/lounge, a kitchen with a table big enough for just 2 people, and off the hallway a pair of side-by-side bedrooms, one big and one small. On the next floor up, at the very top of the house, was the tiny attic room right under the gable, with its dusty window looking out across the city. This he used as his office and den.

Parking his car in the garage built into the ground floor, Pieter dragged himself wearily up the stairs.

Preparing a quick microwave meal, he grabbed a bottle of beer from the fridge and went up to the attic, squeezing his frame through the narrow doorway.

The small room was basic, just an old wooden desk near the window on top of which was an old PC. Against a back wall was a tatty couch, the upholstery full of holes, which sagged every time he sat in it. Covering the floor was a square and threadbare rug. Cobwebs were strung from the roof joists. The place could do with a good clean and a lick of paint, but Pieter thought that would spoil its charm, and anyway he liked the musty smell. Some nights he came up here to do a bit of work or to sit and read under the room's bare bulb. He even sometimes liked to just sit in the dark to gather his thoughts. But tonight he was just too deadbeat to do any of these things. Instead he slouched on the couch and ate his food, drinking his beer from the bottle. His body ached, and he rubbed and massaged the back of his stiff neck, wondering if he had pulled a muscle during his ruckus with Bart.

Finishing his meal, Pieter put the plate to one side and pushed himself to his feet with a groan. Taking his beer, he strolled over to the room's grimy window and looked out across the rooftops of Amsterdam.

Overhead, the clouds parted briefly, revealing the full moon.

He slept fitfully, disturbed by vivid dreams.

He was trapped in a dark and square room, a room that had no windows or doors. He lay naked on the floor, and when he tried to rise something cold and slick moved beneath him. He reached down and recoiled in horror when his hand touched the surface, for it slithered and squirmed. Looking closely he saw that the whole of the floor was a broiling mass of glistening black snakes, twisting and coiling and spitting, their bodies slimy and sticky. Again he tried to climb to his feet, and again he couldn't. Instead, his body started to sink into them, the nest of snakes so deep that in seconds his arms and legs and chest disappeared below the surface with just his face poking out.

And when he looked up in desperation, Pieter saw that the walls and ceiling were also bristling with them, every inch covered with their grotesquely moving bodies.

He screamed a silent scream, and they even slid into his mouth and down his throat, and finally he was pulled down into the hot and fetid darkness.

Pieter woke with a start.

He lay in his bed covered in a sheen of sweat, the covers twisted into knots by his thrashing body.

Staring into the darkness, remembering the nightmare, wondering briefly if he was coming down with a fever because his body ached all over.

He put these thoughts to one side, because something had woken him, and he didn.t think it was the dream.

Listening hard while he held his breath, the sound came again. The creaking of floorboards from overhead, coming from the attic which was directly over his bedroom.

Slowly sitting up Pieter craned his neck and looked up at the ceiling, as though doing this would reveal to him the source of the sound. Even though he already knew what it was. Because it wasn't the noise of the old house settling, the wooden beams groaning and shifting. What he'd heard was the sound of quiet footsteps coming from upstairs.

Pulling back the damp bedsheets he slipped out of bed and padded barefoot across to the bedroom door. Quietly he eased it open. The window on the landing allowed streetlight to cast a soft glow inside, enough for him to see the open door and the narrow stairs that led to the attic.

Again the sound of movement, and this time a faint shimmer of light from a torch.

Shit. He had an intruder.

Moving slowly so as to make no sound, Pieter carefully crept into the corner of his bedroom and opened the cupboard door. He reached inside for a weapon. Contrary to what the public believed, Dutch cops did not keep their firearms at home – in fact strict gun laws also made the ownership of private guns more or less impossible – so instead he took hold of his preferred method for dealing with unwanted visitors. A wooden cricket bat.

Thus armed Pieter moved cautiously across the carpeted landing and paused at the foot of the attic stairs. Whoever was up there was now moving things around, probably deciding what to take, which was a puzzle really because the intruder would have broken in through the ground floor but had for some reason by-passed all of the other expensive items such as the car and smart TV and so on, and gone all of the way up to the attic room where there was virtually nothing worth stealing. Assuming he was alone, and his mates weren't ransacking the rest of the house below. Certainly there seemed to be nobody else on this floor at least.

Pieter decided he could ponder about that later.

His main concern was catching whoever was up there. And now that Pieter had the only escape route covered there was no way out for him.

Feeling more emboldened, but with his heart racing all the same, Pieter started a careful ascent of the narrow wooden stairs.

Thinking it best to not give away his approach, Pieter passed by the light switch on the wall without flicking it, and climbed around the bend, and steeled himself to jump out with a loud shout, brandishing his weapon.

At the last second something must have given away his approach, perhaps no more than a shift in the air, for there was a pause in the sounds from the attic, followed by a sudden rush of footsteps. Two strong hands grabbed him, one on his shoulder and the other on his face, and shoved hard, sending him tumbling back down the steps. He didn't fall far but ended up in a heap at the bend in the stairs, and he quickly scrambled up, all attempts at stealth now abandoned.

Bursting through the doorway, gripping the cricket bat in both hands, Pieter yelled fiercely. A quick, split-second glance showed him the room was empty, but when he looked over towards the small window he had the shock of his life.

Someone clad in a black coat or cloak was squeezing through the tiny opening, using it as a way out. Whoever he or she was, they were quite small in stature (for a crazy moment he was convinced it was a child) but it was still an effort to get their frame through, and they wriggled about with one leg still dangling down inside the room. Sitting half in and half out, the figure turned and looked back over their shoulder at Pieter. And when he saw the face, alabaster white with deep-set, shadowy eyes, his heart nearly stopped. The grin that appeared was like a narrow black gash.

Momentarily shocked, and unable to fathom the idea of anybody desperate enough to risk escaping this way, four stories above the street below, he nonetheless quickly regathered his wits and dashed across the room, his bare feet crunching over something on the rug, and made a lunge for the foot.

He missed it by inches and the intruder slipped through the opening.

Flinging the cricket bat away Pieter reached up for the edges of the window frame and pulled himself up, squirming his upper body through, and anger flooding his mind. Stupidly he looked down, seeing the street and canal far, far below, and a wave of vertigo overcame him.

He almost keeled over the edge and just in time he managed to grab a hold of the wooden joist and winch sticking out from the gable above his head.

Twisting awkwardly about, Pieter looked across the steep rooftop towards the next house over. The black-clad figure was scrambling up and over the roof tiles like some frightful phantom of the night, coat tail flapping in the breeze. Reaching the apex of the roof, they paused and looked back at Pieter once more.

Their eyes met briefly, those twin black pits seeming to bore straight through to Pieter's brain.

Still clinging on to the wooden joist, he watched as the figure disappeared into the night.

CHAPTER 7

FAMKE AND THE STUPID OLD FOOL

Dropping back down to the floor inside the attic room, Pieter could feel himself starting to shake from the after effects of the terrifying incident, and so he paused to allow his nerves time to settle.

The room was in darkness but with a mixture of moonlight and orange streetlight filtering through from outside, his eyes quickly adjusted to the gloom. Looking about, he was able to see that everything was as it should be: nothing had been disturbed or moved, the room wasn't ransacked.

Shaking his head in confusion Pieter drew a deep breath and turned and pulled down the window sash. Then, picking up the cricket bat once again, he crossed back over the room, heading for the staircase.

He paused halfway as he again felt his naked feet crunch over something on the floor rug. Looking down he strained his eyes and tried to make out what it was, and then stepping carefully around, he quickly moved down the stairs, flicked on the light switch, and hurried back up.

Standing beneath the bare light bulb Pieter searched the floor. He saw the brown powder scattered over the rug, and his own footprints where he had stepped through. Kneeling down, he scooped some up on his fingertips and examined it closer. Soil. It was soil.

Unable to work out what the hell was going on, Pieter went back down to the landing below. Putting on all of the upstairs lights he went from room to room, checking to see if anything was missing or disturbed, and also to make sure nobody was still lurking about. He looked in all of the wardrobes and cupboards, beneath the beds, in the shower cubicle, tried all of the windows to see if any had been forced open (unlikely this high up, but he did it just the same) and then moved down to the floor below which he hardly used really, and repeated the process. Finally he found himself on the ground floor. The front door was still bolted on the inside. He opened it and looked up and down the street, feeling the night time chill as he was only wearing boxers, went back inside, and then passed through the door into the ground floor garage. His car was still there and untampered with and the automatic garage door securely shut with the alarm still activated.

There was nothing amiss anywhere. Nothing seemed to have been stolen or even so much as moved. No doors or windows were damaged. All apart from the window right at the very top of the house.

The least likely scenario seemed to be the only plausible one: that the intruder had entered the house the same way in which he had left. And that was just too crazy to think about.

Pieter trudged back up to the third floor. He should call this in, have the place dusted and swiped for fingerprints.

He walked into his bedroom and was reaching out to pick his mobile up off the nightstand when it rang, the vibration making it dance across the surface.

Scooping it up he checked the display – **Unknown Number** – and the time, which was shortly after 4.30am. Nobody called at that time unless it was bad news. He swiped the green answer button.

Before he even brought the phone to his ear he heard the hysterical screaming, which chilled him to the bone. There was then some incoherent shouting, then more screams, and at last a woman's voice, repeating over and over, "Your dad, your dad, Hansje! Hansje!!"

"Famke?"

More screaming, louder and louder.

*   *   *

When Pieter pulled up at the Westerdock ten minutes later the police divers were just hauling his dad's body from the river.

In the pre-dawn greyness the flashing lights of the emergency vehicles cast an eerie glow across the scene, and he stayed sitting in the car, watching as they heaved and manoeuvred the corpse up the high river wall and onto the pathway. Using ropes and pulleys attached to a fire-engine, the knot of men and women laid his dad prostrate and then covered him with a white sheet.

Further along the roadway was an ambulance with its back doors open. Inside he could see Famke sitting with a red blanket around her shoulders and talking with a paramedic. Her long grey hair was soaked and her lined face was a mask of pain and grief. Pieter felt nothing for her. His mind was blank.

After a few minutes he noticed the distinctive figure of Daan Beumers break away from the cluster of figures and head his way. Pieter had no idea how the sergeant had heard about the incident, but he was here.

Opening the front passenger door his friend climbed in next to him. They sat in silence for a minute.

Finally, just to break the silence, Beumers said, "It's a fucked up world."

Pieter nodded. "Full of stupid people."

Out on the river was his dad's houseboat, anchored mid-stream. Two figures wearing bright orange life-preservers moved about on the wooden deck. Alongside it was a police launch.

"I warned him, a thousand times. Not to go out there."

"Well it seems they'd been drinking," the police sergeant told him. "All day long, according to his friend."

"I know," Pieter responded simply.

Beumers turned to look at him closely, perhaps to gauge how he was handling the situation. But Pieter kept his face blank, unwilling to give anything away, instead choosing to keep his own counsel.

"We're still putting the pieces together, which isn't easy as she's in a complete state and probably has mild hyperthermia to boot. And she's also still a little drunk. But what we know is that your father, Hansje, decided he wanted to do a spot of fishing and so the pair of them took his boat out there –"

"In the middle of the night?" Pieter cut in sharply.

"Famke says that your father said that was the best time to go, through the night. That's when they bite the most. The fish. She tried to stop him, or at least that's what she has told us, but he insisted. And so she tagged along with him. Anyway, they carried on drinking, did a bit of fishing, getting drunker and drunker. The blokes out on the boat," he nodded at the figures on board dad's houseboat, "they've found a load of empty cans and bottles, enough for them to be pretty sozzled. Anyway, somehow your dad fell or tripped, or maybe the boat was rocked by a heavy swell, and he ended up in the water. Famke jumped in after him and tried to get him out, but it was dark and she couldn't find him… After that she managed to climb back on board, and rang you…"

"The stupid old fool. After everything he's gone through, in Bosnia and in and out of rehab, to die like this."

"I know mate. The post mortem will confirm her story and everything."

"Just one of those things, eh?" Pieter answered back somewhat unfairly, and then he climbed out of the car and walked over to where his dad's body lay on the pavement. Beumers caught up with him, and a hush descended amongst the police and rescue people, for they all knew who Pieter was.

Crouching down, he peeled back the edge of the sheet and looked down on his dad's face. A heaviness seemed to descend on him, crunching him on the inside, pressing his soul down and down.

He stood and walked silently away.

Pieter went straight back home.

The city was just starting to come to life around him but he barely noticed during the drive. A strange tingling sensation was gently vibrating through his body which he knew was the onset of delayed shock, mostly a result of seeing his dad like that and the implications of the whole sorry affair. He also guessed it was partly due to the break-in and subsequent fright it had caused. Oh, and not forgetting his confrontation with Bart. All in all the last few hours had been one long shit-storm of emotions, so much so that he felt physically and mentally exhausted.

Parking in the garage, he locked up and set the alarm and then went back up to the third floor. The house was silent and still and felt empty, but he carried out the most cursory of checks in each room just to be sure the intruder hadn't paid a second call. He was too weary to fret about it just yet, and to be honest he didn't care too much one way or the other. For the same reasons, he'd chosen not to mention the break-in to his colleagues. Nothing had been taken or damaged, and he also wanted to think about the incident first as there were aspects to it which he just couldn't fathom. But now wasn't the time.

There was no point in going back to bed. He wouldn't sleep anyway, even though he felt drained. Instead he made himself a strong coffee and sat at the small table in the kitchen. Watching the sunrise through the lace curtain, Pieter went over events.

The tragic passing of his dad, horrible and wretched as it was, nonetheless somehow felt preordained. His life over the last twenty-odd years had been one of steady decline, through a failed marriage and family feuds and booze, everything intertwined and twisted into a mess of bad choices and stupid mistakes, with it all stemming from his time in Bosnia. Pieter had moved heaven and earth to intervene, seeking help wherever he could find it, but all of the programmes and rehab that his dad had gone through – some of it unwillingly – had ultimately come to naught. And deep down inside, Pieter had always known this was how it would end. Not necessarily with his dad dying, but in a failure of his dad's willpower. All of the time and effort thrown back into Pieter's face.

He thought back to the previous afternoon and that brief glimpse of his dad and Famke in Leidseplein Square. Wondered whether anything he could have done differently might have made a difference. Instead of driving on to rush to Lotte, perhaps if he'd climbed out of the car? Taken his dad home to get him sobered up? Would he still be alive now? Or would it have merely delayed the inevitable?

Even as he contemplated these things Pieter knew it was a pointless exercise. None of it would change what had happened. Blaming himself for his dad's own self-destructive personality would only let guilt eat him away inside.

But he still felt empty and hollow to the pit of his stomach.

His thoughts and ruminations were interrupted just then by a call on his phone. He answered it. This time it was Daan Beumers – did he ever sleep? Pieter wondered.

"Hey mate. I've been asked by the powers-that-be to tell you not to come in today. Actually, with it been Saturday tomorrow I reckon you should have the whole weekend off. We can handle things here for a few days."

"Yeah ok Daan. I guess it make's sense."

"If there are any major developments with the case I promise I will be straight on the blower to you. We should be getting the results on the British victim sometime today, so I will email you the details, but there's no need for you to go over it too much. And the same applies to your father. I'll make sure he's taken care of."

Pieter suddenly felt shattered. He sagged in his chair and felt his eyelids grow heavier by the second. Perhaps 40 winks wouldn't be out of the question. And then over the weekend, not only would he make arrangements with his dad's passing, but he was also determined to investigate the strange circumstances of his early-morning visit by the intruder, and the bizarre nature of his escape through the window.

Saying goodbye to Beumers, Pieter lay his head on the table and was fast asleep in seconds.

*   *   *

He woke up sometime towards mid-morning feeling much more refreshed and invigorated. Grabbing a quick shower and eating a bowlful of fruit with yoghurt, Pieter switched on the coffee machine and instead of waiting for it to bubble to a slow boil he popped down to the ground floor and stepped outside.

Between his house and that of his neighbours there was a short, covered passage leading to a small courtyard where someone had arranged some potted plants. Pieter headed down the passage and stood with his back to the wall so he could look up at the side of his attic room, which was perched right at the top of the sloping roof four floors up. The window itself was around the front, but he could just about make out the roof slates and the side of the bell gable, as well as part of his neighbours adjoining roof.

A pipe fed out from a small hole in the wall, just about where the bathroom was in Pieter's house, and dropped straight down to a small grate in the ground next to where he was standing. There was also a small ledge below the bathroom window, perhaps two or three inches wide. Above this there was nothing but a flat and featureless wall, until the attic dormer itself. About fifteen feet with no hand-holds or ledges or pipes or anything whatsoever to grip or climb up. His neighbour's side was pretty much the same but without even a pipe. So there was no way the intruder could have climbed up to his attic window from this location, unless he had rubber suction pads on his hands!

Could he have got in via his neighbour's house, waited until she had gone to bed, and then scrambled across the roof to Pieter's? Possible, but from what he knew the old dear never used the top floor of her house and access to her attic was sealed off inside with a brick wall. So very doubtful.

Pieter considered the possibility of the intruder breaking in from below. But most homes in Amsterdam – including his – had no basement as they were prone to flooding. All there was down there was some recent concrete foundations and the original and very old wooden piles. It was a real puzzle.

Strolling back around to the front he paused and looked at his garage door. Perhaps the intruder had hidden in the boot of his car at Police HQ and stole a ride right into Pieter's garage? Not possible: not only would he have set off the car alarm when sneaking out of his hiding place late at night, but he would also have had to pass from the garage through the connecting door into the house itself, triggering that alarm as well.

Ok, so whoever had been in his house last night cannot have entered via the attic window, not unless they had somehow found a route up to the roof perhaps from a house further along the row and then travelled across many rooftops to climb in through his window? Short of checking with each of his neighbours, there was no way to be absolutely sure, but it still seemed unlikely.

He guessed a really good cat-burglar would know how to by-pass a good security system and get past the house alarms, but then again why go to all of this trouble to break in but then to leave empty-handed? Unless robbery wasn't the motive? But if the intention was to harm the occupant – and if the intruder knew who Pieter Van Dijk was, he could have a motive for wishing him harm – then he'd had ample opportunity to sneak into his bedroom and attack him whilst he had been sleeping. Yet he hadn't.

So, let's see, Pieter thought, using his policeman's analytical brain.

Motive No 1: Robbery – Nothing seemed to be missing so he ruled that one out.

Motive No 2: To harm, or murder, the sleeping homeowner – Again, he could tick that off the list.

Perhaps there was a Motive No 3: Not to steal anything, but to leave something behind?

He remembered the soil up on the attic rug.

Finishing his coffee and quickly clearing away the breakfast things, Pieter searched around under the kitchen sink and came out with a small dustpan and brush, as well as a small plastic container. Then he slogged up the narrow stairs to the attic room.

Kneeling on the square rug he once again studied the brown powdery substance. There was lots of it, more than he had realized last night. There were small piles and heaps of the stuff. Certainly more than would be accidentally walked in off the soles of somebodies shoes. It actually looked to have been deliberately placed there, apart from the bits which his own feet had scattered and trod into the rug. And in amidst the brown there seemed to be flecks of a black tarry substance. Pieter ran his fingertips through it, feeling it gently. It felt and looked like ordinary soil to him. But when he brought his fingers to his nostrils and sniffed, he detected a familiar briny smell. Like seaweed?

Utterly confused, he spent several minutes sweeping up the mess and storing it safely away in the plastic container. First thing Monday morning he would get the guys in the lab to analyse it. Hopefully they would provide some answers to the mystery.

Done, Pieter grabbed the chair from beside the small desk and PC and, placing it on the floor, climbed up and shoved open the sash window and poked his head out of the attic. He looked down at the street below, once again struck by how high up this part of his house was. The guy last night – and he only assumed it was a man – certainly had a pair of balls for the method of his escape was treacherous and foolhardy, for one false step in the dark and he would have taken a swan-dive straight down to the pavement below.

Shaking his head in wonder, Pieter reached out his hands and felt around the outside of the small, square window frame, along the bottom, up the sides and across the top, searching for a tell-tale sign that the window had been jimmied open from the outside.

Nothing. Not a single thing.

*   *   *

After lunch Pieter decided he ought to go over to his dad's houseboat to collect a few things. As he fancied a bit of fresh air, he decided to walk.

It was a sunny day and the thirty minutes it took to go from his home on the Singel canal to the riverfront helped to clear his head. Before reaching his dad's, there was a small jetty that he stopped off at. It was nothing more than a stumpy wooden thing sticking out into the river for a few metres, but he stood there and let the stiff breeze blowing in off the water ruffle his brown hair and blow away a few cobwebs.

The houseboat was tied up in its usual spot, having been brought back to the riverside by the police once they had finished their work. Two cheap fold-out deckchairs plus dad's fishing gear was still up on the top, together with a large number of empty cans and bottles of booze. Finding some plastic refuse bags, Pieter cleared away the rubbish and then packed away the fishing rods and tackle back into their storage space just inside the boat's narrow entrance.

Going into the main living space Pieter stood looking at the usual mess, the place cluttered with junk and old furniture and unwashed cups, but somehow empty and soulless. He hated the thought of throwing a lot of it away, but really who the hell would want it? Pieter planned on selling the houseboat itself, quickly and if need be, cheaply, just to get it off his hands. Some of the better items, such as the kitchen stools and the small bookcase in the corner, perhaps the double bed, and the TV which was one of those smallish but modern flat-screen ones, they could probably be sold with the boat itself. After all, who would want to buy an unfurnished and empty houseboat? But much of the rest was no use, they were simply things that dad had accrued over the years and allowed to fall into a state of disrepair. Junk really. As for dad's clothes, he would go through them and take the better items to a launderette and offer them to a charity organisation.

However, Pieter didn't have the energy to make a start today. Perhaps later in the week, during his evenings, he would begin the sad process of dismantling his memories of his dad, bit by bit loosening the connection his dad had with life. Until eventually, all traces of him would be gone, having made no mark whatsoever on the world.

There was one thing that Pieter wanted to salvage today, however.

He stepped across the room and took down the framed photo from the wall, the one with his dad and his army colleagues. Holding it in his hands, Pieter looked at the image, and could not stop the lump in his throat. He clenched his teeth, realizing that this photo right here was a snapshot showing the point in his dad's life when his entire future altered. The moment that signified the start of his gradual decline, from a happy and kind father and dedicated soldier, to the grubby and sordid nature of his addiction, and the tragically sad circumstances of his death. All caught in this one photograph, frozen in time.

Tucking the picture frame under his arm he set off for home.

When he reached his canal house he found Lotte sitting on the doorstep.

"Can I come in?" she asked.

CHAPTER 8

SLEEP OVER

She'd brought with her a large canvas shoulder bag, presumably with a few overnight things inside. Plus a bottle of Sauvignon Blanc.

"I don't want to be on my own," she'd told him, talking quickly "Call me silly, but I just can't bear the thought of spending another night there, jumping at every sound. Which is stupid, because nothing actually happened there, but it's still frightening thinking that Bart might just turn up. Even though you said he wouldn't."

She'd smiled up at him sheepishly from the doorstep.

"And I don't think you should be on your own either," she'd added.

Then Lotte had jumped to her feet and flung her arms around him, squeezing him fiercely. Crying, not for herself, but for Pieter and his dad, who she had never even met.

Inviting her in, Pieter led her upstairs. On the way up she had a good glance around his place, her disposition now a little sunnier, and her positivity starting to rub off onto him as she nodded approvingly at the set up.

When she walked into his kitchen however, she stopped in her tracks, and looked at him.

"A microwave and a small toaster? Seriously, that's all you have?"

Pieter shrugged.

Rolling her eyes, Lotte handed him the bottle of wine. "You open this, and find some glasses. I'll see what I can rustle up." With that, she began going through his cupboards.

A short while later they were sitting side by side on the couch in the living room and tucking into cheese and ham omelettes sprinkled with pepper, their plates resting on their laps, the bottle of wine with two glasses on the coffee table. The TV was on, showing some silly comedy movie starring Robert De Niro, but the sound was turned way down so that they could talk.

Pieter told her all about life with dad. About his own upbringing as a boy growing up in Zandvoort on the coast during the 1980's, some of which she knew from their chats, and about his dad's time in Bosnia and the subsequent boozing and violence, most of which she knew. Then he gave her a brief rundown on today's events, about the phone call from Famke and his dash over to the houseboat, the recovery of his dad's body from the river. The dull acceptance that the tragedy seemed almost destined and preordained, regardless of whatever help he had tried to give him. Towards the end, Lotte reached over and took his plate, placing it on the coffee table with her own, and then leaned into him with her arm stretched across his chest, snuggling into him with her face.

Pieter pondered on whether to tell her of last night's intruder, but quickly decided this would be unwise. The last thing he wanted was to freak her out and send her running for the hills. And besides, he liked her company.

They finished off the wine and watched a bit more TV and then Pieter told her of the sleeping arrangements. She could have the big bedroom while he would make up the single bed in the smaller bedroom for himself. Lotte briefly looked up at him through her blonde fringe, the way she did, and wriggled her eyebrows mischievously, before grinning and nodding.

It had been a long and stressful couple of days for them both.

With a quick kiss on his cheek, she said night, night, and skipped off to bed.

*   *   *

For a second night running, his sleep was disturbed by more bad dreams.

This time he was walking down an endlessly long, wooden jetty, through dense fog. To either side the grey sea was choppy and stormy, even though there wasn't a breath of a breeze. Everything was in monochrome, and totally silent.

On and on he walked. Glancing down, he saw that his feet were naked and dirty, like he had walked for days and days, and he felt the rough wood of the jetty scrape and chaff the bare skin.

After an age, he noticed the dim outline of a man standing before him. He had his back to Pieter and was at the end of the jetty, looking out at the stormy sea. Slowing down, Pieter came to a stop.

"Dad?" he asked, his voice echoing in the foggy silence.

The figure, really just a dark outline of a person, did not respond.

"Dad, is that you?"

The person started to turn slowly, the shoulders and head coming around, until Pieter could see the face. But there was no face, just a large, black smudge where the features should be. Not a hole, just a shadow. And out of this ghastly countenance spewed mud and blood, in an endless stream of vomit.

Pieter turned to flee in terror, but arms reached around his sides to embrace him, and the two of them toppled backwards into the water.

Another dream.

Something heavy on his chest, pressing down so that he could hardly breathe, with soft hands on his body, stripping his clothes away, and despite the bone-chilling coldness of those hands, he became erect, and lips closed over him.

The gentle knock on his door roused him from his slumber. Pieter glanced across at the alarm clock, seeing the time was just after midnight. After a slight pause, there came another light tap on the door, and then it opened a few inches.

Lotte slipped into the room dressed in her nightie and stood by his bed, looking down at him. In the moonlight filtering in through the curtains her face was a pale oval.

"I can't sleep," she simply told him.

Pieter hesitated for a moment, and then lifted the covers.

Lotte climbed into the bed beside him, and they lay gently embraced in each other's arms, quietly crying together. Eventually they slept.

*   *   *

They awoke to the sound of bells ringing out from Westerkerk

"I am so savage, I am filled with rage, Lily the Werewolf is my name. I bite, I eat, I am not tame. My werewolf teeth bite the enemy. And then he's done and then he's gone. Hoo, Hoo, Hoooo!"

RADIO WEREWOLF BROADCAST, 1945.
PART OF JOSEPH GOEBBELS PROPAGANDA MACHINE.

OPERATION CARNIVAL

THE CITY OF AACHEN IN OCCUPPIED GERMANY.
MARCH 1945.

The mission had gone wrong right from the start.

By early 1945, as the Allied noose had tightened around Nazi Germany, Hitler, Himmler and the German leadership had become increasingly desperate to stave off defeat. In an almost final throw of the dice they had launched the fiercely loyal and utterly dedicated Werewolf Commandos at the Americans, Canadians and British approaching from the west.

Their role was to infiltrate enemy lines to carry out acts of espionage, sabotage and assassinations, to sow the seeds of confusion and mayhem, to launch ambushes against enemy supply columns. To bring terror to the allies. To delay the inevitable defeat for the Fatherland. Operation Werewolf.

Swift Strike II, led by Commando Unit No 1, was to conduct possibly the most daring of these operations. Codenamed CARNIVAL their task was to assassinate *Burgermeister* Franz Oppenhott – the Mayor of Aachen, recently selected by the Americans as the pro-western new leader of the city after it fell to the Allies in late 1944.

Commando Unit No 1 was led by Herbert Wenzel, with the ever loyal Joseph Leitgeb as second-in-command. She-wolf Ilse Hirsch, the female assassin who had continued to train with them for the past few months, was also part of the team, as was the young 16 year old crack-shot cadet Morgenschweiss. The final two members were Hennemann and Heidorn, both former scouts who knew the area around Aachen like the back of their hands, and who had chosen various rendezvous points and safe houses for the operation.

They had left on March 20th, flying in a captured B-17 Flying Fortress, which took them over enemy territory. On reaching their drop-zone, the commando unit had parachuted out and landed safely in the quiet evening countryside, and quickly gathered up their gear. Up to that point everything had been progressing exactly as planned, but within minutes of landing things had quickly started to unravel.

Moving swiftly away through the woods they had picked up a trail and followed it towards their first planned overnight resting place, a disused loggers hut. But before reaching their destination they had stumbled upon a courting couple in a small clearing, literally running into them.

With screams of panic and shouts of confusion, a desperate fight had broken out as the two had tried to escape, and so taking matters into her own hands, Ilse Hirsch had stepped forward and shot the man in the head at point-blank range with her tiny pistol. More chaos ensued, and somehow in the pandemonium the woman had got away, fleeing naked into the woods and leaving her dead lover behind.

As if this wasn't bad enough, it soon became clear on checking the man's corpse and belongings that he was a border guard from the local provost unit, and would be soon missed. Probably even before the woman could raise the alarm, his colleagues would be out looking for him.

Wenzel quickly told two of the team to carry the body deeper into the trees and dispose of it, to try and cover it with branches as they didn't have time to dig a grave. When this was done the team hurriedly pressed on, now led by the local scouts who insisted it was too dangerous to keep following the track. Instead they cut a path through the woods, hoping that they would provide good cover.

With twilight descending they eventually made it to the ramshackle old hut. It was too risky to light a fire and so they settled in to sit out the long and cold night, constantly on edge in anticipation of discovery.

Dawn arrived the following morning signalling a sunny, early spring day. To their huge relief the night had passed without incident. They rose and ate a miserable breakfast of hard tack biscuits washed down with water. Afterwards, with the men watching, Ilse Hirsch removed her green coveralls and changed into a blouse and skirt. Young Morgenschweiss ran his eyes hungrily over her figure as she changed, something she paid little mind to but which Wenzel noticed.

The plan was simple. She would go ahead of the others and make her way into Aachen alone. She had a contact there, an old friend from the League of German Girls, who knew the city well. She would show Hirsch the house where their target, Franz Oppenhoff, lived. Hirsch would watch the building and the comings and goings of the staff, to try and get a good understanding of their daily routine. In the meantime the rest of the commando unit would move forward on to their next hiding place, a safe house in a suburb of Aachen itself. Later that day Hirsch would re-join them. Then they would wait for the right moment to strike.

Hirsch prepared to leave. At the last moment she insisted that the 16 year old boy travel with her part of the way, just until she reached the outskirts of the city. There was still people out looking for them, she reminded Wenzel, patrols no doubt searching for the missing border guard, and she had no wish to risk discovery without help. And despite his age he was the best-trained sniper in the group and so it made sense. Annoyed at this small but last minute change of plan, Wenzel nevertheless reluctantly agreed.

He watched them disappear into the thick woods.

Hirsch pushed on at a quick pace with the boy following behind. She could feel his gaze on her at every step. She had no qualms about being able to defend herself if discovered, that was just a story she'd given to Wenzel, but the boy was becoming a problem, just as she had anticipated during their training during the winter. So the solution was simple and would not take long, and after they had travelled perhaps half a mile she stopped abruptly and turned to face him. Hitching up her skirt she told him to be quick, and so he hurriedly undid his trousers and eagerly did as she said. When he was done she sent him hurrying back to the others.

Reaching into a small pocket hidden inside the hem of her skirt Hirsch took out a tiny glass vial and removed the stopper. Squatting down on the ground she let the boy's seed drain from her into the bottle, and then returned the stopper. In a few days she would have her period, and she would add her menstrual blood to the sperm.

*   *   *

With the information gleaned by Ilse Hirsch during her casing of the home of Franz Oppenhoff the team decided to make their move several days later.

The weather had turned, and March 25th was a cold and wet day. They waited until late in the afternoon before Wenzel, his second-in-command Leitgeb, and one of the scouts, Hennemann, left their hiding place and made their way through the city. Hirsch, the 16 year old and the other scout would stay behind and ready their escape route out of Aachen.

Burgermeister Oppenhoff lived on the corner of Eupener Strasse and Heidweg, in a large house set back from the tree-lined street. Hennemann was instructed to wait on the corner, lunchbox in his hand and smoking a cigarette and looking like any other worker on his way home. Wenzel and Leitgeb strolled confidently through the high wrought iron gates and rang the doorbell. They waited a moment, and then the door was pulled open to reveal the housekeeper and a small infant girl, presumably one of Oppenhoff's children.

With a smile Wenzel asked if they could see *Burgermeister* Oppenhoff. They had workers passes which needed to be signed by the Mayor, as they had expired. He and his colleague worked for the *Organisation Todt* labour force carrying out important construction works on the border fortifications, so it was necessary that their paperwork was in order. Happy to oblige, the housekeeper and child went to find the Mayor.

Franz Oppenhoff appeared several minutes later, pleased to see the two visitors but querying whether it was polite to call unannounced at such a late hour? Wenzel apologized and reached into his pocket for his workers pass.

But instead he pulled out a handgun, a silencer-equipped Walther automatic, and levelled it at Oppenhoff's face. Breathing heavily, Wenzel scowled at the man before him. His hand started to shake, his whole arm quivering, and he suddenly felt light-headed, his lips going numb, and he was sure he was going to be sick.

Seeing his commander hesitate Leitgeb reached across and took the gun. "Heil Hitler," he whispered, and pulled the trigger.

They fled back out of the front entrance and through the gates, and then turned and raced down the street towards where Hennemann was waiting on the corner. Seeing them coming, their lookout nodded – the way was clear – and then he turned and strolled calmly away into the evening gloom, whistling to himself.

Wenzel and Leitgeb ran straight across Eupener Strasse, narrowly avoiding being hit by a passenger trolley trundling past, and climbed over the railings along the pavement. On the other side was a steep slope covered with thick bushes and undergrowth. They careened down without slowing. At the bottom was a narrow stream, which they raced along, the cold water splashing up in their wake. This small tributary would feed into another beck, and this in turn would lead them out through the city suburbs to the safe house. If all went as arranged Hennemann would join them later.

Wenzel and Leitgeb made it safely back in the early hours of the following morning, and Hennemann several hours later.

Their escape along the waterway had taken much longer than planned, as parts of their journey took them in and out of the city sewer system, through culverts and drains. Finding their way in the pitch dark, with rats and stray dogs for company, was only a part of the problem as well. Very quickly after the assassination the whole of Aachen had been put on high alert, and an immediate curfew imposed until dawn. Anybody found on the streets without authorisation was subject to immediate arrest by the American occupying forces and their German collaborators in the civil guard. This had forced them to take frequent halts during their flight, waiting until the coast was clear and hoping the enemy patrols with their guard dogs did not spot them. Eventually, exhausted and stinking of raw sewage, they had stumbled through the back door of the safe house.

It soon became clear that during their absence something had happened. The atmosphere was tense and everybody was on edge, as though they had arrived in the midst of an awful argument.

The main cause of it seemed to revolve around Erich Morgenschweiss, the youngest member of the team, and Ilse Hirsch.

The teenager had become infatuated with her. The whole team had noticed his behaviour over the last few days, following her around, offering to perform any small task for her. Yet nobody had realized just how obsessive he had grown until last night, when she had made a point of ignoring him and even belittling him, laughing in his face and calling him her 'little pup'. Very quickly her spurning him like this had changed him from a quiet and almost timid boy into a brooding young man, sitting in the corner and throwing angry looks at her. The atmosphere had grown increasingly tense. Quickly an air of bitterness developed, with Georg Heidorn, the second local scout left behind, finding himself caught in the middle. He guessed correctly that something must have occurred between them at some stage but wisely he chose not to voice his thoughts out loud.

Eventually a huge row had developed and Hirsch and Morgenschweiss had nearly come to blows, only the return of Wenzel and Leitgeb, and later Hennemann, preventing a violent confrontation.

Wenzel snapped. He told the whole team that their behaviour was putting the whole operation under threat. Yes, they had successfully carried out the assassination, but they still had to make their way back east to friendly lines. Nothing would be allowed to jeopardize that. Angrily he instructed them all to get some rest. They would be leaving in a few hours.

Later that evening, as they were gathering their things in readiness for their departure, young Morgenschweiss went outside to collect some kindling from the small barn at the end of the narrow garden. Ilse Hirsch slipped out after him.

Seeing them leave, Wenzel watched through the window as she followed him down the overgrown path.

Several minutes later she came back into the small downstairs room where the other members of the team waited. They looked at her, then at the door behind.

"He will no longer be a problem," she informed them, as she washed blood from her hands.

The remaining five members of the commando team successfully evaded the patrols and fled quietly into the surrounding forest without capture, quickly leaving Aachen behind.

Hirsch led them, an unspoken acknowledgment that she was in command now. Nobody raised their voice in protest at this subtle change as an air of fear gripped them all. Each one of them now petrified of this strange and alluring woman in their midst. This She-wolf.

They made good progress on the first day. As pre-planned they struck out north-east towards a small hamlet about twelve miles from the city. Here they spent the night sleeping in an abandoned mineshaft where supplies of food and ammunition had been left by fellow partisans. On the morn they continued with their escape, making for the castle at Hulchrath, but sometime during the afternoon disaster struck.

They had come to the edge of the woods and paused to look at the wide field ahead of them. On the far side were more trees leading off into the distance. They needed to get across soon if they were to keep on schedule, and so after waiting for several minutes to make sure that the way was clear, they all rose from their crouching positions and made a dash for it.

Half way across Hirsch failed to notice the thin strip of wire stretched between two fence posts, and as her foot pulled it clear there was a huge blast as the tripwire triggered the grenade buried in the ground. She fell to the ground clutching her leg, and Leitgeb's jaw was blown clean off in a spray of gore. He twitched a few times and then lay still.

Hirsch's injury would not be fatal, but with her leg broken and torn open she could not carry on. As the three remaining men gathered around her she looked at them in turn, her face twisted in agony. Then she reached out and passed her small knapsack to Wenzel.

"Get to the convent. You know what needs to be done."

CHAPTER 9

WEREWOLVES

On the Sunday morning they walked to Dam Square and caught the tram out to Vondelpark, where they had lunch in the Blue Teahouse. Afterwards they enjoyed the warm spring sunshine. On the Monday morning Pieter thought it was time to get back to work, and so Lotte decided she would spend the day looking for a new job and a place to live (one which Bart didn't know about). Pieter told her there was no rush and that she could stay as long as she needed.

The first thing he did on arriving at HQ was to arrange for a motorbike courier to take the soil sample he'd retrieved from his attic floor over to the NFI forensic lab in The Hague. He marked it as PRIORITY so hopefully the results would be back first thing tomorrow and possibly sooner. Having done this he went up to his office and set to work catching up on developments.

There he found a message from Daan Beumers written on a post-it note stuck on his PC monitor. The sergeant was working on trying to get the security cam footage from the corner café enhanced, but in addition he had two more sets of cameras that may have caught the suspects fleeing from the murder scene at the outdoor urinal. Everything was on a file attached to an email which he'd sent over to Pieter. Finding the file, Pieter dragged it to his desktop and clicked.

The three sets of footage showed the same thing from three different angles. The first – and most interesting – was from the café, featuring Henrietta and Maarten cosying up on the bridge with the shadowy form of a fleeing person racing by. Exactly like Beumers had done several days earlier he played it back several times, and as with his colleague he could not help the shiver run down his spine, like someone dropping an ice-cube down his back.

The other two cameras were from the doorway of a store selling kinky leather gear, one pointing up the alley towards the bridge and the other aimed down the opposite way. The first angle also showed the same bizarre figure fleeing at breakneck speed, but this time hunched over and with its head angled down, perhaps aware of the cameras. The second one had this person – and from its diminutive size it certainly appeared to be a child – rushing headlong down the alley before quickly disappearing to the right, onto the parallel canal there.

The young couple, Henrietta and Maarten, were both adamant that there had been three people fleeing, one slim adult and two kids. But none of the footage showed the other two suspects. Having been down that alley many times over the years Pieter knew there were a number of other even smaller passageways branching off from the main one, snaking deeper and deeper into the creepiest parts of the red-light district. The area was like a rabbit-warren, dark and dangerous for the unwary. In all likelihood the suspects had split up and disappeared for good.

Let's hope Beumers could get the footage enhanced and sharpened up, perhaps enough to pull a reasonable image of the suspects face.

Next Pieter took a quick and rather cursory glance at the autopsy results from the Oliver Monroe murder, which didn't really show anything totally unexpected. The guy had all sorts of drugs in his system: a fair quantity of cocaine and Tangerine G13 weed, plus some phencyclidine angel dust – the usual party drugs that lots of tourists and visitors to Amsterdam enjoyed. He had also recently had sex as there were traces of condom spermicide on the remnants of his penis, plus traces of semen inside his underwear. Once again, nothing unusual in that.

The injury to his scrotum was the only significant wound, other than bruises and light abrasions probably as a result of a brief struggle. The cut through the testicles had been done by a blade with a serrated edge – ouch! – and would have resulted in huge blood loss, followed quickly by unconsciousness and death. The scrotum itself had been recovered as Beumers had indicated at the time.

His hotel room had revealed nothing of interest. Staff there confirmed he was a regular guest, and also that he often returned late after the main doors were locked for the night. Checks on his hotel key cards showed he accessed the elevators and main doors at various times in the early hours, so it seemed that during his regular business trips to Amsterdam he thoroughly enjoyed the night life. Again, no surprise. In the meanwhile his wife back in London confirmed she was well aware of his cheating, but confided that she kept this knowledge to herself for the sake of their marriage and the small child they had.

Pieter briefly broke away to make himself a coffee, standing in the doorway of his office to stretch his legs. It was already mid-morning, and his back ached from sitting slumped in the chair, but it was good to be working. The distraction from the weekend's events was good.

Back at his computer he decided to see if anything had come through from ViCASnl regarding the dragnet he had ordered for the symbol and message that had been daubed on the wall near the Mila crime scene. Disappointingly nothing had been red-flagged on the national database with links to any known Level 1 crimes throughout The Netherlands, however there was a hit on the Interpol system. The symbol was apparently used by a Hells Angels group in Finland during the 1970's and 80's, a bunch of ultra-violent psychos who specialized in attacking Asian shopkeepers who refused to pay them as part of their protection racket. They had links to other far right groups such as COMBAT 18 in the UK, and although their crime spree was going back several decades it might still be worth checking out. Also, this reminded Pieter of the silver finger ring with the Norse script, found at the Monroe crime scene.

Time to pay Adolf another visit.

Pieter found him down in his bunker – sorry, basement room.

"Hey buddy," Floris greeted him, looking up from the book he was reading.

Pieter noted the title: **UNIFORMS AND INSIGNIA OF GERMAN ARMED FORCES – 1914 to 1945**. More books were spread out over his desk, all of a similar nature.

"Adolf," he smiled back.

"Sorry to hear about your father."

Pieter pulled over a chair and picked up one of the volumes, and flicked through it, snatching glimpses of black and white photos, maps, colour plates. "You been doing your homework?"

"I certainly have," Floris told him with a big grin. He reached across and pulled out a sheaf of papers, and waved them about like a winning lottery ticket. "These are print-outs of the photos I took of your mystery ring. I spent yesterday going through my books, and have managed to pinpoint exactly what it signifies." He looked pleased as punch.

"Don't keep me in suspense Adolf. You might just be about to crack the case."

Floris rocked back and forth, his body shaking from mirth, or at least that's what Pieter hoped, and not from his illness.

Laying the photos over the desk, Floris turned his book around in a flourish and showed Pieter the double-spread illustration. A colour drawing matching the ring that was found on the ground next to Oliver Monroe's castrated body, down to every detail.

Pieter leaned forward for a closer look.

"What you are looking at," Floris informed him, "is the signet ring given to members of an elite unit of World War Two-era German commandos. The ring was sometimes referred to as a wolf's angel. The men – and women – who wore it were named Werewolf Commandos." He tapped the W in the book illustration and then in the corresponding photo on his desk.

"Werewolves?" Pieter looked at him dubiously, but he was thinking about the message on the wall.

"Yes, but not of the furry wolf variety that bay at the full moon. These were highly-disciplined soldiers drawn from the SS or even the Hitler Youth and trained in all aspects of specialized combat. Infiltration, sabotage, reconnaissance, assassination, hand-to-hand fighting, that kind of thing. They were a little like the *Brandenburgers*

Special Forces outfit but at a whole new level, and their job was to deploy behind enemy lines and sow confusion and fear in their ranks. They were ruthless, fearless and totally loyal to the Third Reich. This was real heavy stuff."

"And they each wore one of these?" He pointed at the illustrations in the book.

"That's right, when they passed out each soldier received one. They were solid silver. I'm still working on the script etched into the side, but I'm guessing it's some kind of motto."

Pieter picked up one of the photos and studied it closely. "Is this an original?"

"No. But it is a near-perfect modern reproduction. You see the hallmark here?" Floris tapped at the image. "This gives us the town mark – in this case Amsterdam – as well as the duty mark and the date, which was nearly two years ago. It also contains the makers mark."

Pieter raised his eyes from the photo to look at Floris.

Pushing a slip of paper across his desk Floris told him: "I've written down the silversmith's name and address."

Taking the note, and the photos, Pieter rose.

"See you later Adolf."

On his way out through the main entrance he grabbed Daan Beumers who was just arriving.

"Morning Boss, I was just on my way up to see you. Those CCTV stills are getting cleaned up nicely-"

Pieter cut him off. "Tell me later. You're coming with me."

*   *   *

Levi Kohnstamm was short and fat, with a bald head and a grey goatee beard which gave the impression that his head was on upside down. The black suit he wore was at least two sizes too small. Perched on his nose was a pair of tiny pinch-nez spectacles.

His silversmith and jewellery premises were out in the Jordaan District just west of the inner canal ring. It was a tiny two-room place squeezed onto the upper floor above a bakery. The main outer office, where he met his clientele, consisted of a large oak desk in front of three deep-set leaded windows overlooking Rozengracht Bridge. To each side of the windows were a pair of matching display cabinets containing silver plaques, trophies, silverware, and a chessboard with silver pieces. On the corner of the desk, suitably arranged and within easy reach of any would-be customers, were a pile of glossy catalogues.

In the corner of the room was another door, locked with a key-pad security system. Presumably this was the inner-sanctum, where the real work was done.

Kohnstamm was busy weighing some silver jewellery on a set of digital scales, making notes in a little black notebook, tutting and shaking his head occasionally, and so Pieter and Beumers waited patiently.

After several minutes like this, during which Beumers especially was starting to fidget and sigh, Pieter coughed politely.

"Oh yes. Inspector..?"

"Van Dijk, Amsterdam PD."

Kohnstamm carefully closed his notebook and set it aside, and replaced his pen into its silver penholder. "You were enquiring about some rings. To sell or to buy?"

"Neither." Pieter reached into his pocket and pulled out the photos he'd borrowed from Adolf. He passed them over. "We are after any details you may have regarding these."

"Which you made," Beumers added gruffly.

Kohnstamm had a quick glance at them and then handed the photos back. "Mmm, mmm, indeed," he replied through pursed lips.

"So you definitely made these? For a customer?

"I most certainly did. Beautiful aren't they?"

"You do know what these are don't you?" Beumers asked, his brow furrowed.

"I didn't ask for the why's and where fore's. None of my business really. Clients commission me to do all kinds of work all of the time.

It could be to repair some family heirloom, to design a piece of body-piercing for some young teenage tearaway hippy. Or to craft a bespoke piece of jewellery like this." He pointed vaguely at the photos of the ring.

"So this particular ring? With this somewhat unique design? You remember making this specifically?"

"Yes I do Inspector. I remember clearly that it was around about eighteen months ago. The circumstances were slightly unusual, which makes it stick out in my memory."

Pieter and Beumers exchanged a look. "How so?"

"Because it was all very hush-hush, and shrouded in secrecy. Very exciting in a way. The client wished to remain anonymous. I arrived for work one morning to find a long letter shoved through my letterbox, with a very precise request detailing what was required, the design and nature of the work. There was also a large amount of cash, with a promise of more to follow once the items were finished. I never once had any face-to-face interaction with the client themselves."

"So you're saying you don't know who this mystery person was? No name or anything? Even though they just handed over a huge amount of money?"

The jeweller said nothing, just shrugged his shoulders helplessly.

"How much are we talking?"

Kohnstaam turned his eyes on Beumers. "Oh about twenty thousand euros."

"For a fucking ring?"

"Not just one ring, err, Sergeant. The order was for over thirty."

They were both quiet as that sunk in.

Kohnstaam shuffled about in his chair, beaming at them. He removed the pince-nez spectacles and rubbed the bridge of his nose, and then carefully put them away in a slim leather case.

"I'm very sorry that I can't be of much help officers. I really don't have much to tell you. The client placed a commission and paid in cash, half in advance and the rest afterwards. When the work was complete I was instructed to leave the rings in a safety deposit box at DNK just down the road on Prinsengracht. At no stage did I see or speak to anybody. Like I told you, it was all very hush-hush."

"Do you still have the letter and envelope?"

"I'm sorry. I don't keep my paperwork after a commission is complete. Client confidentiality and all that."

Pieter and Beumers rose to leave. At the door, Beumers turned back. "You're Jewish right?"

"Of course."

"How do you live with yourself, knowing what those rings are? The kind of people who ordered them?"

Kohnstaam laughed lightly. "Work is work Sergeant."

As they headed down the stairs, they heard the jeweller add, "and beggars can't be chooses."

"Fucking creep," Beumers declared once they were outside. "Did you see the way he was drooling when he was talking about teenage hippies having their belly buttons pierced?"

"Now now Daan. Perks of the job."

Pieter strolled up the street to a nearby tobacconists stand. He bought a newspaper and re-joined his colleague.

"You checking the soccer results?"

"I'm not, but you are." He shoved the newspaper into his hands, and nodded at a bench across the pavement. "Park yourself down there and keep an eye on our friend here. Follow him wherever he goes, make a note of anybody who calls around to see him. Report back if anything odd happens."

"What, you putting me on stakeout?"

"Yes. I know it's below your paygrade Daan, but at least you'll be getting plenty of fresh air."

From his office window Levi Kohnstaam peered down at the figure sitting on the bench below, ostensibly reading a newspaper.

Keeping well back out of view, but not taking his eyes off the police officer, he reached across and picked up the telephone receiver from his desk. He knew the number by heart, it was ingrained on his brain, and his chubby fingers quickly tapped at the buttons.

Listening to the ringing sound at the other end of the line Kohnstaam's throat went dry. He dreaded the times he spoke to the person he was now calling, for it filled him with a terrible stomach-churning fear, but he knew he had no choice. On the fifth ring, it was answered.

"Is something wrong?" said the gravelly voice.

"I uh… mmm, possibly," he stuttered. "I've just had a visit from the police. They were uh… asking questions, about the rings."

Silence, except for the faint buzzing on the line.

"I thought you should know. One of them is still outside, wa-watching my office. What should I do?"

Again there was a long pause, but now with the sound of laboured breathing. Finally a response.

"Come here. Let him see you. Make sure he follows."

The line went dead.

CHAPTER 10

A WALK ACROSS TOWN

From where he was sitting Daan Beumers had a good view of Kohnstaam's office. Beside the bakery was the narrow door that led to a short passage and the staircase leading up to the second-floor premises, and he could see the three windows above, lit up from the inside. He could not fail to see anybody coming or going.

He waited for nearly an hour, with no movement. Sitting and holding his newspaper, legs crossed and hunched down on the bench, Beumers hoped he did a good impression of someone casually passing time. After a while, he laid the paper down and stretched one arm out on the back of the bench, looking all nonchalant, but with his eyes fixed on the building across the street.

After a while, with nothing happening and his empty stomach starting to rumble, he contemplated dashing over to the nearby kiosk to quickly grab a sandwich and a coffee. He would still be able to watch the doorway, and he would only be gone for two minutes. Yet just as he was about to get to his feet the decision was made for him. The office light suddenly blinked off and the three windows went dark, and Beumers' body stiffened in anticipation.

Sure enough, about a minute later the narrow door opened and out stepped the distinctive form of Levi Kohnstaam.

Now dressed in an overcoat over his ill-fitting suit, and with a black leather briefcase in his hand, the portly jeweller paused briefly as he locked the door, and then set off, waddling his way along the pavement in the direction of Rozengracht Bridge. Beumers waited until he was about fifty metres or so in front, and then rose and followed.

Kohnstaam turned onto the bridge and crossed over, the large tower of Westerkerk looming overhead. He continued on down the busy thoroughfare of Raadhuisstraat, passing over several more canals as he headed in the direction of Dam Square.

Beumers matched the jewellers pace, keeping a steady distance behind but not wanting to let him get too far ahead and risk losing sight of him in the busy streets. He wondered whether to call Pieter Van Dijk, to let him know their man was on the move, but he decided to wait and see exactly where he was headed first, or whom he was planning to meet with.

The large edifice of The Royal Palace came into view, marking the end of the road, and Kohnstaam veered across the pavement and skirted around the corner of the large grey building. Beumers lost sight of him temporarily and he hurried forward, hoping to catch up, and then to his relief caught a glimpse of him again as he cut a diagonal path across the cobbles of Dam Square.

The jeweller was a fast walker for such a large man, his legs moving like pistons, and Beumers thought perhaps he was hungrily making for one of the hot-dog stands, but instead he bustled by them and then dashed across Damrak, weaving in and out between the trams and bicycles.

Again Beumers lost sight of the waddling figure and he swore under his breath, thinking maybe he had been seen, but when he followed across the busy street he soon spotted him again, going by the large obelisk of the National Monument and turning left down the narrow pedestrianized Warmoesstraat.

This was the edge of the red-light district and where most of the gay bars were located. At this time of the afternoon it was starting to get busy, and Beumers had to dodge around people just to maintain visual contact with his target. Once more, he was impressed with the fast pace Kohnstaam was setting. Perhaps he had a rendezvous with a boyfriend? Or was about to turn down Saint Annenstraat to enjoy an afternoon with one of the window girls? It wasn't unusual to see men suddenly pick up speed as they neared their destination here.

But Kohnstaam instead continued on straight down the street, head down and briefcase swinging. At the far end there was a sharp turn to the right, or alternatively there was a teeny little passageway that continued straight on, and the jeweller chose the latter. Somewhat hesitantly, Beumers followed him into the narrow passage.

His nose wrinkled at the smell of stale urine, the cobbles here always in the shade and puddled from underground seepage from the sewers. Halfway down the alley had a slight kink, and then thankfully re-emerged back into daylight, and Beumers found himself stepping out by the side of St Nicolaaskerk Cathedral. He was just in time to see Kohnstaam slip around the far corner.

Jogging along the pavement Beumers sneaked a look around the side of the wall. Kohnstaam was just disappearing down some steps alongside a familiar-looking building, which was perched over a canal.

He finally relaxed, for there was nowhere else for the jeweller to go. He had reached his destination.

Standing there and breathing hard after the quick walk across the city centre, Beumers studied the short, circular squat building ahead of him. This was The Weeping Tower, or Schreierstoren to give it its proper name. Beumers knew a little about the place as it was a well-known landmark to locals if not the tourists. It was part of the old city defences, and the spot where in centuries past the womenfolk came to wave off their husbands as they set sail on riggers and whalers, crying quietly to themselves as they watched the sailing ships depart.

A few years ago Beumers knew the place had been renovated and turned into a trendy bar, but more recently it had shut down and from what he understood was now empty again. There was one entrance on this side, a solid-looking, old door at the top of a short flight of stairs. Above this, and set at various intervals in the building's round walls were a number of square windows. The roof was squared off, but atop this and looking like a witches pointy hat was a steep triangular slate turret.

Looking back at the door Beumers noticed it was padlocked on the outside, and Kohnstaam hadn't used this entrance anyway, instead he had descended the steps to the side. Down there, Beumers knew there was an old wooden deck down at the canal-level, and beside this was a small boathouse underneath the stone tower itself. There must be a way into the building down there.

Leaning against the wall from his vantage point, he fished out his mobile and dialled a number. Pieter answered on the first ring.

"I think we might have him Boss"

He quickly told Pieter everything that had happened, the journey across the city, and where Kohnstaam had ended up.

"Schreierstoren?" Pieter asked in confirmation.

"Yes. He's still inside now."

"Are you sure he didn't spot you tailing him?"

"He had no idea. He was in too much of a hurry to notice anything."

Still holding the phone to his ear, Beumers continued to stare at the building, thinking hard. He heard Pieter's voice come through the phone again.

"Wait there. Don't go inside until I arrive with backup and-"

But Beumers cut the call, and moved out from his hiding place.

In his office at Police HQ on Elandsgracht, Pieter stared at his silent mobile phone in horror. He quickly pressed the call-back button and listened in dismay as it went straight to voicemail, which meant either Beumers had switched off or he was already inside the building and wouldn't be able to get a signal.

Jumping to his feet he snatched his Walter P5 from its secure metal box and slipped it into his waist-belt holster, and then rushed out of the office, bellowing for some backup.

Beumers walked quickly down the narrow street, the slight incline passing the main entrance, and stepped through a small wooden gate. A narrow flight of wooden stairs led down the side of the building to the small deck below. Tied up there was a long motor launch with a wooden cabin. There was no sign of anybody, everything was still, but he nevertheless felt his heart starting to race as he withdrew his sidearm. Gripping it in both hands he kept the barrel pointed down, and with his left shoulder brushing the brickwork of the building he carefully descended the staircase.

Only twice previously during his fourteen years in the police had he been required to draw his gun while on active duty, and he'd never actually had to fire it. Preying that today would be no different he moved slowly down one step at a time, his mouth suddenly dry, his breath coming in quick rasps.

At the bottom he moved along the deck and paused just this side of the entrance to the boathouse. Counting silently to three, he swung quickly around the corner, arms outstretched and pointing the gun dead ahead. Swinging from side to side to cover the interior, quickly establishing there was nobody here, and then casting his eyes over the small speedboat floating inside and seeing this too was empty. He breathed a sigh of relief and took a moment to get his bearings and scan the layout of the boathouse.

The speedboat was in the centre with its bow pointing towards the building's wide entrance. There was a walkway around the inside walls of the boathouse, going down the side, then across the back behind the boat, and then along the opposite wall where it led to an open doorway. Hung on the walls were a number of fishing rods and nets, plus a life-ring. In the far corner was an empty deckchair, and beside it a steaming mug of tea or coffee.

Treading as quietly as he could, Beumers followed the walkway around, thinking perhaps coming in alone wasn't the wisest of decisions but knowing it was too late to change his mind now. Drawing to a halt near the doorway he snatched a quick look before pulling his head back out of sight. Still nobody. Just another set of steps leading upwards.

Once again, he moved as quietly and slowly as possible, but this time going up into the main building itself.

At the top was a large and open room. There were several windows down both sides, letting in bright sunlight from outside, allowing him to take a good look.

There wasn't much to see as the room was mostly bare. He guessed this must have once been the main bar area but now all of the fixtures and fittings had been ripped out, the furniture all removed, the floorboards were all covered in a layer of dust and pieces of crumbling plaster from the walls. High on one wall was an old ship's figurehead, a naked woman's upper torso, leaning out and leering down at him. Apart from this and a couple of shallow alcoves beside the gutted fireplace, there was nothing.

Except over in the far corner was an iron spiral staircase, twisting around and up before disappearing through the roof to the upper level. Which meant that Kohnstaam, together with whoever he had been in such a hurry to see, must be up there. There was nowhere else where they could be.

Taking several deep breaths to fortify himself, Beumers started out across the room, his firearm once again pointing forward.

Passing beneath the steady gaze of the figurehead, he didn't notice the man standing upright in one of the alcoves, he only heard the scrape of footsteps after he had gone by, when it was too late.

Something came down over his head, and a pair of huge hands held whatever it was in place, and when Beumers opened his mouth to yell in fright and realized he couldn't draw in any air, or breathe at all, he knew it was a plastic bag. A terrifying panic gripped him, and he brought up the gun, but just as he was reaching backwards to fire at the person standing behind him, another person came into view, the face all distorted and pale-looking through the plastic bag. Then he was punched hard in the stomach and what little air he had in his lungs was expelled, the gun flew from his grasp, and something was being coiled around his neck, cinching the bag tight, either a rope or a belt. The inside of the bag misted up, and each time he tried to suck in, instead of oxygen he sucked in the plastic into his mouth.

Thrashing and kicking, Daan Beumers felt consciousness slipping away.

CHAPTER 11

THE WEEPING TOWER

Pieter slammed on his brakes and the car slewed to a stop by the corner of St Nicolaaskerk Cathedral. Seconds later a pair of patrol cars, each with two police officers on board, came to a halt on either side.

Ahead of them was the huge bulk of Schreierstoren tower, all brooding and silent. There was no sign of Daan Beumers, and Pieter could only prey his colleague hadn't been foolish enough to go in by himself. On the journey over, as he'd gunned the engine and drove straight through several stop lights, he had tried phoning once more. The result was the same: no answer. With a sick feeling in the pit of his stomach he stepped out of the car, his sidearm still in its holster on his hip, and waited while the other officers joined him.

"Ok guys, let's do this nice and quietly. Sgt Beumers might be in there, and hopefully he's made an arrest and will be the big hero, but until we know for sure what's happening we show extreme caution. But let's not ignite the situation if we can help it." He looked at them each in turn. "Understood?"

When he was sure they were ready, Pieter led them down the gentle slope towards the main entrance.

Something caught his eye then, a sudden movement above. Glancing up he caught a quick glimpse of a figure up on the flat roof of the squat building, moving behind the crenelated wall, before suddenly dropping out of sight again. Pieter paused, calling for the others to halt, but as they turned to look in his direction the figure popped up again, holding something in both hands.

The air erupted with thunderous noise. There was a series of violent explosive sounds, the very sky seeming to shake with a horrible *brrrrrrr!* And then the roadway disintegrated in a cloud of sparks and dust, there was a horrendous scream and two of the police officers went down in a spray of blood.

Pieter knew instantly what the sound was. A hail of bullets had just ripped into the small knot of men, bringing chaos and furious pain, and Pieter dropped to the ground in an instant. There was a moments pause, and then another burst of gunfire, longer this time, hitting the prostrate men again. The shots halted, and then a third burst shattered the air, this time coming from a different spot up on the roof. Pieter risked a quick look, seeing a second figure up there, both gunmen popping up and down to fire again and again.

"Get back! Behind the cars!" he screeched, the order directed at himself as much as his colleagues, and he scrambled across the tarmac on his stomach. He reached his car and yanked open the driver's door and crouched into the shelter it provided, drawing out his sidearm. Over to his left he saw two other officers doing likewise behind their own patrol car, one of whom had a red bloom of blood spreading across his blue shirt. Down the slope, the two who had been hit in that first violent burst lay in the roadway, perfectly still, and Pieter had little doubt that they were dead. Somewhere behind him, on the busy road and bridge that crossed the canal, there was total pandemonium, with pedestrians screaming and fleeing in terror, and cars and bicycles weaving this way and that.

Pieter turned to wave them back, shouting at them to get away, to get down, but even as he did so he watched in sheer terror as the gunmen opened fire once more, this time aiming deliberately towards the bridge. There was a tram crossing, trundling along and unable to alter course, and then the sides of the vehicle were ripped apart as the bullets struck, with sparks and glass and metal flying in all directions. There were more screams, and the tram came to a shuddering halt, with smoke and flames starting to curl from beneath its chassis.

"God no," Pieter moaned, and then he reached into the car and grabbed the mike. Thumbing the switch he bellowed, "Code Red, Code Red, Zodiac! Prins Hendrikkade Bridge outside the cathedral, multiple-shots fired! Officers down, C's down! Taking heavy fire!! Multiple gunmen, number unknown, firing from Schreierstoren tower! All units respond, Code Red!"

Another burst of gunfire cut him off, this time the rounds riddling the patrol car where the other two officers were sheltering. They hunkered down even more, their eyes bulging in sheer terror.

Once the firing paused Pieter sneaked another brief look, just long enough to see a third figure with a gun, this one aiming through one of the square windows just below the roofline.

Fuck! Pieter thought to himself crazily. They had fucking assault rifles, possibly Uzi's or C10's from what he could see, real military grade stuff. Where the hell, where the fucking hell did they get those from? And even as he watched, something much worse happened. One of the men up on the roof pulled his arm back and then threw something small and round through the air, like a cricket ball, but when it hit the ground and bounced along in a series of metallic *clinks* Pieter knew instantly what it was and flung himself down just as the grenade exploded near the second patrol car. The ground shook, bouncing him up off the surface, and gravel danced just above the tarmac, and with a tremendous rush of hot air the police car exploded. Pieces of red-hot metal billowed out, scything outwards, but his own car sheltered him from the worst thankfully. Shaking his head to clear it, he looked in amazement at the fiery wreck of the car.

A sudden fury built up inside him, a wild hatred, and Pieter raised his gun. Resting his wrist between the car's doorframe and the open door itself, he aimed the Walter P5 at one of the figures on the roof of the building and fired two quick shots, the gun kicking hard. The shots struck the stonework, missing their target, but the silhouette of the gunman at least dropped from view. Encouraged by this the two other officers, one of them wounded, withdrew their own guns, and commenced firing. Their shots were slow and steady and precise, a testament to their training, and Pieter felt ridiculously proud of their coolness.

If nothing else their return fire might at least keep the gunmen's heads down, but the situation was still dire. There were civilians badly in need of help, and probably a number of them were dead, and from the look of it the tram was now well and truly ablaze. But Pieter knew if he made an attempt to dash across to the bridge he would be hit. Pinned down like this they were trapped and unable to offer any help. In addition two of his men were dead, one more wounded.

He tried to think, but more prolonged gunfire from the tower made this impossible. The sound was beyond anything he'd experienced before, a roar of brutality, and he thought perhaps he was screaming in madness but wasn't sure as the whole world was one huge cacophony of noise. Another loud explosion rocked the ground, and then non-stop automatic fire.

How many were holed up in there? At least three, but then he noticed more pandemonium on the far side of the canal towards the old docks, so he assumed there were more gunmen opening up on that side of the tower as well.

They had to do something quickly, otherwise they would have a massacre on their hands.

*　　*　　*

In the distance Pieter could hear the sound of sirens approaching but decided they could not afford to wait. Somehow he had to hit their flank and also draw their fire away from the bridge. The only way to do that was to get down the incline, past the tower itself. He knew there was a small deck down there on the canal side so presumably there must be a way into the building from there. If he could get down there he might perhaps hit them from behind, pin them down until help arrived.

Pieter crouched low and crawled around the back of his car, and then down to the front passenger door. He was sheltered from the gunfire on this side, but just a few feet away was the burning wreck of the second patrol car, and the heat of the flames was nearly unbearable.

Yanking open the passenger door and keeping his head down, he reached across the seat and released the car's handbrake. Withdrawing his body, Pieter waited until gravity started to take effect, and slowly his car gently started to roll forward down the gentle slope of the street. Closing the door again, he kept pace with the vehicle, now well sheltered from the gunfire spitting out from the tower.

The angle of his car glided it diagonally across the cobbled surface of the road, the front heading towards the low wall beside the gate and stairs leading down to the deck. It was only travelling slowly and it crunched into the stonework with only a slight bump, not enough to smash right through the wall itself. Thus embedded in the wall the car now gave him some perfect cover, and he leaned across the bonnet and looked up towards the gunmen on the roof, who were busy firing down towards the bridge in the opposite direction.

Then he noticed that indeed, there was a fourth man firing through a window on this side, his shots hitting targets on the far side of the canal. Pieter could clearly see him framed in the open window, as of yet unaware of Pieter down below.

Kneeling down and using the car's bonnet as an armrest, he took careful aim, the gun's sights centred on the gunman's chest. He squeezed the trigger twice, there was the double kick, and then the figure was hurled backwards and fell from sight. A satisfied flush spread through Pieter's chest, and his face was set in grim determination.

More long bursts of gunfire shattered the air once again, and he turned his attention to those up on the roof. The two men up there continued to pour heavy fire down towards the roadway and bridge, raking any target they could spot, but from where Pieter was he was gratified to see that most of the civilians had fled or found good cover. What's more he saw the familiar sight of a police personnel van skidding to a halt near to the flank of the cathedral. The back doors flew open and out poured a phalanx of heavily armed assault police. Pieter knew these were equipped and trained to deal with this exact scenario, and they moved rapidly and fluidly with perfect precision, finding cover wherever possible, and immediately opened a heavy return fire towards the tower. Within seconds the building was shrouded in dust and smoke kicked up by their rounds, and the very earth shook under the power and violence of the gunfight.

Another squad of police arrived. With the gunmen inside the building pinned down, this second team dashed forward to the main entrance, and using a battering ram they soon gained entry, lobbing in several flash-bangs to clear the entranceway before they piled in. The gun battle moved inside, the explosive sounds now echoing and reverberating from within the enclosed space.

Pieter felt his heart rate start to slow a little, and he came to his feet somewhat unsteadily. But just as he thought things were getting a little more under control the sound of a loud engine caught his attention and he glanced down towards the deck below just in time to see a small speedboat emerge from the boathouse, turn onto the canal at full speed, and race away. On board he counted three or four people, all clad in dark clothing and heavily armed. Without giving himself time to think, Pieter raised his gun and aimed, then fired at the fleeing target.

The round missed, he saw a spout of water fly up just in front of the boat, but it was enough to startle whoever was at the controls, making them yank at the steering wheel. The boat twitched, and the sudden movement unseated one of the passengers who fell off the stern and into the water. The speedboat roared away, leaving their man behind.

For a couple of seconds the figure floundered in the water, but he quickly recovered his composure and struck out for the far side of the canal, making for a steep ladder fixed to the side of the wall. Pieter watched as he reached out and grabbed the bottom rung, then hauled himself up, drenched in water.

The gunfight in the tower sounded to be nearing the end, with just single shots ringing out as the police assault squad began mopping up the last of the holdouts. Again making a snap decision, Pieter raced back up the slope and past the burning police car, then turned right to run full-pelt over the bridge and by the bullet-riddled and smoking tram. Around him he saw dead and wounded civilians lying in the road, but he could not stop to offer them aid, instead he charged past and preyed he could cut off the escaping gunman in time.

Yet even as he thought this he saw just ahead of him the figure emerge from the canal and clamber off the ladder, then race forward onto a second bridge, this one crossing over Oosterdok. It was packed with people, some peculiarly drawn towards the sound of the battle, others just standing as if frozen with terror. The gunman charged through the crowds, pushing and screaming at them, which sparked even more fear as they tried to move clear.

Pieter followed through the crowds, holding his gun high and shouting for them to get away, and he emerged on the far side having lost sight of his quarry. Pausing on the corner, he soon saw him, running alongside the dock and heading east, no doubt hoping to escape in that direction. There were fewer people here, and the man was fast, already racing at full speed down the long, straight quayside, with the large expanse of water on his right and the huge, modern library building on his left. Pieter set off in pursuit again.

A cold wind blew across the open dock, buffeting against Pieter and whipping up small waves on the water. There were a few boats moored here, mostly pleasure crafts, but most of the larger ones were at the very far end where the museum haven was, and because the location was slightly off the beaten path for tourists there were thankfully very few people around. Which was good as the gunman was still armed, Pieter seeing what looked like a small snub-nosed Uzi strapped over the running figure's shoulder. He was also probably feeling increasingly desperate, abandoned by his fellow gunmen, and with a cop on his tail, so who knew what actions he would take to stay alive and escape?

To make this clear to his pursuer the black-clad gunman turned and fired a short burst towards Pieter. The rounds went high, and the few people about scattered and ran. Pieter ducked and stayed back, keeping his distance, but when the man spun away and continued to run Pieter followed once again.

Half way along the quayside was the large Chinese restaurant, permanently moored on its floating island out on the water. He thought perhaps the gunman might run up one of the narrow gangplanks and begin shooting people inside, but no, he ran straight on by, Pieter noticing the small faces of the diners within pressed up against the windows and watching events in amazement.

On they went, Pieter feeling increasingly winded and wondering how long he could keep this up. There was no sign of his quarry slowing at all. Somewhere he thought he could hear a helicopter but it was hard to be sure because of the strong, gusty wind.

Finally they came to the end of the quayside. Crossing the water here was a wide footbridge, linking the dockside with the roadway and the tunnel passing beneath the river Ij to the north shore of Amsterdam. Above the tunnel was the peculiar science museum with its rooftop café terrace. Pieter followed as the figure crossed over. Halfway across the bridge had a small turn and as he rounded the bend another burst of bullets came his way, tearing up the metal handrail inches from his chest.

He waited a moment, using the pause to get his breath, and when he risked a quick peek he saw the man he was pursuing jump down off the far end of the bridge and turn sharply to the right, running alongside the steel flank of the museum. Pieter raced after him.

They ran by the old ships and barges moored at the jetties. Sitting in his chair, a fisherman watched them, and then calmly went back to his fishing.

Further along, where the museum ended, eight lanes of traffic *vroomed* into the cavernous entrance to the road tunnel, and here the escaping figure clambered over the retaining wall and dropped down to the road. Pieter went to follow, then saw that it was an eight or nine foot drop. He didn't have time to take the longer route right around the incline, and so he gritted his teeth and jumped. He landed hard, the impact jarring his knees, but nothing twisted or tore, so he picked himself up and ran out into the busy lanes of traffic. Cars and vans screeched to a halt or weaved around him, and horns blared angrily, but Pieter ignored them and prayed for a miracle. Just ahead the figure had made it over and was running along the opposite pavement, turning his head to see how close his pursuer was.

Seconds later, having made it in one piece, Pieter sprinted down the narrow path with the oncoming traffic just inches from his right shoulder. He watched the gunman twist and disappear around the wall, and moments later he did likewise.

A long flight of steps climbed up the gentle sloping roof of the science museum, leading to the rooftop café terrace, and the man was all but sprinting up them like he was the bionic man or something. Already near to exhaustion, Pieter watched him in dismay.

"You've got to be kidding me?" he gasped and panted to himself. This man was relentless.

Pieter started to climb.

He'd only been here once before, with his then wife, to spend a pleasant couple of hours drinking beer. Under normal circumstances it was a fantastic location with probably the best views out across Amsterdam's skyline. Yet this was anything but normal, and as he hauled himself up the steps he knew in the back of his mind that the gunman had made a bad mistake. For once at the top, with the only way back down being via these same steps, he would be corned with nowhere to go. He could take a hostage of course, a situation that Pieter fervently hoped did not happen, but ultimately he was trapped. It was this thought, this end result – taking him down and arresting him – that drove Pieter on for the last few strides.

Finally reaching the top, he looked around.

The rooftop terrace was built in a series of wooden stages, each higher than the previous one, like wide, ascending platforms. It was meant to represent the deck of an old sailing ship. The café itself was right at the top. Around the edges were a number of viewing spots with observation binoculars, and beyond them some handrails. And beyond that, a two-hundred foot drop straight down to the water below.

The man he'd been chasing was standing by the handrail, staring out as though admiring the view. He was alone. Anybody else up here had had the good sense to run once they saw his firearm. Behind the man, far off in the distance, Pieter could see Schreierstoren tower shrouded in smoke. The sound of the helicopter from earlier was louder now, and glancing up he saw it swing into view, hovering just above them. Its side-door was open, and a police marksman was leaning out with his sniper's rifle pointing at the gunman.

Raising his Walter P5 and pointing it at the man's back, Pieter approached slowly, hesitantly.

When he was a dozen or so feet away he stopped.

"It's over you fucker!" he shouted. "You've nowhere to go! Put the gun down and turn slowly around!"

The man did not move or reply.

"Do It! Or that guy in the chopper will blow your fucking brains out!!"

Slowly the head turned.

To reveal not the face of a hardened criminal or terrorist, but that of a young teenage youth, a boy of perhaps fourteen or fifteen.

Pieter gawped at him, completely thrown by the revelation and what it meant. A child! They'd been using a child to gun people down!

Then the boy smiled at him, a menacing grin that seemed to taunt Pieter.

Turning back to the handrail, the youth climbed up and dropped away into the abyss.

CHAPTER 12

DYATLOV

Pieter staggered, partly from the downdraft from the helicopter, but mostly from shock. He reached out and grabbed a hold of the handrail where moments before the boy had been standing.

Raising himself up he leaned over and looked down but all he could see was the grey water far below. Twisting about he raised his arm and signalled the crew on board the chopper, which then spiralled out and downwards, where it hovered a few metres above the surface of the dock. The rotor blades pushed at the water in a circular pattern, creating a mini squall, and it commenced gliding back and forth as they began a search.

Pieter moved away and slumped down onto one of the wooden benches. In his mind he saw once again the boy's face and his ugly smirk, and he cast his mind back to the night the intruder had broken into his home, and the brief moment their eyes had made contact. He knew, he was absolutely sure they were one and the same people. But this time, instead of making good his escape, rather than be captured he had made the terrible decision to jump to his death.

God, what kind of people were they dealing with here? Had the boy been so brainwashed that dying like that was preferable to imprisonment? And could he, Pieter, have done something to prevent it? If he'd known how young he was, he might have held back, maybe not even pursued him so determinedly. Yet the ruthless nature of these people was apparent from the gun battle back at the tower. He doubted if any of them were willing to be captured alive. And did they deserve to be, considering what they had done, to Mira and Monroe… and maybe to Daan! Jesus, in all of the uproar over the last thirty minutes he had completely forgotten about Sergeant Beumers.

Grabbing his mobile he rang HQ and asked to be patched through to whoever was in command back at the tower. A gruff voice came on.

"Dyatlov, make it quick."

"Inspector Van Dijk here. Have you finished over there?"

"Van Dijk, I've been looking for you, where the hell are you?"

"Over at the science museum, but never mind that. Are there any survivors inside the tower? Sergeant Beumers was in there."

"I can see the helicopter from here. Is that something to do with you?" demanded Dyatlov.

"Yes! But listen, is Beumers ok? Is he alive?"

There was a slight pause on the line and in the background Pieter could hear shouting, orders been relayed no doubt. Then Dyatlov came back on, his voice more subdued.

"Inspector, you need to get back here now. There's something you have to see."

The assault-squad leader was a short and stocky man with a severe buzz cut, who was ex-paramilitary from the Russian armed forces. Pieter knew him vaguely, having worked alongside him during a drugs operation a year or so ago.

Dyatlov met him as he clambered down from the armoured police vehicle that had ferried him back from the docks, then led him over the bridge past the wrecked tram and down towards the tower.

Laid out on the road were three rows of body bags, one set marked with small blue flags and the others with red and black flags.

"Nasty business," Dyatlov informed him. He pointed at the row marked in blue. "Eight civilians, but that tally might rise as we have some seriously wounded who might not make it. And four police, your two uniformed officers plus one of my men who died when we stormed the place. The one's in black are the bad guys. Five of those bastards. No prisoners."

"Make that six," Pieter told him, and briefly explained what had happened over at the science museum.

Dyatlov said nothing, merely grunted.

"You said four police? There's only three bodies here?"

"The other's still inside. I'm sorry Inspector, it's your man."

Pieter nodded and whispered, "OK."

The squad leader led him over to the main entrance, where the door was hanging on its hinges. Before following him inside, Pieter diverted across to the line of body bags marked with their little black flags. Bending down, he lifted one of the sheets, seeing the face below was pock-marked with small burn marks on one cheek, but still clearly recognizable as another young teenager.

Pieter reached below and pulled out the boy's hand. He saw on one finger a familiar-looking ring, identical to the one back at HQ. He let the hand go, and stepped through the doorway.

Inside there were signs of severe fighting everywhere. The walls were riddled with bullet holes and the floor littered with glass shards and wooden splinters where the windows had blown in. Hundreds, possibly thousands of copper shell casings were scattered underfoot. Over to the right an opening led to a flight of stairs leading down, probably to the boathouse below, and plumes of black smoke billowed upwards. One whole wall was gone where a grenade had exploded, and several firearms were laid about, abandoned or dropped by the gunmen. And in the far corner a spiral staircase disappeared through the ceiling. He heard voices up there, someone laughing, no doubt members of the assault team on a high after the fierce firefight.

And straight ahead, propped up against an empty fireplace, was the body of Daan Beumers, his head covered in a clear plastic bag. What looked like black tape was wrapped around his neck to shut off the life-giving oxygen. The face a sickly blue colour, with his red-veined eyes staring back at Pieter.

He looked away, his eyes filling up with tears.

You bloody fool, mate, Pieter thought to himself.

Dyatlov gave him a moment to compose himself and then indicated the spiral staircase

"There's another one upstairs on the roof."

Pieter followed him, their boots clunking on the metal steps. The doorway was built into the sloping side of the slate turret that capped the roof, and they stepped out into bright sunlight. They walked around to the far side.

Here, sprawled upright against the turret as though sunbathing, was a man's naked corpse. Its ankles were tied together with a plastic cable-tie, and both arms were pulled up above the head and tied individually with lengths of rope to the weather vane atop the turret, giving his posture a Y-shape. Both eyes had been gouged out and the mouth was a wide, bloody hole, with a trail of red gore down his chin. The tongue had been ripped or cut out.

Daubed in blood across the body's fat stomach was another symbol, different and more intricate than the one found on the alley wall. Some kind of pentagram inside a series of concentric circles, with various strange symbols around the edges, triangles, weird letters with dots inside them or arrows or crosses poking out from them, a crescent moon at the very top

At the corpse's feet was a briefcase, innocuous amidst the debris of battle up here, which Pieter surveyed as he stepped away and looked out over the wall.

"We're not sure if this one's a civilian or one of theirs, so we left him here. He quite obviously died a different way too."

"Oh, he's one of theirs," Pieter replied. He pointed at the briefcase. "I met him earlier, with Daan Beumers. His name is Levi Kohnstaam, a jeweller from The Jordaan. We had him under surveillance. Beumers phoned to tell me he was following him here. But now it looks like he deliberately led him to this place. Led him to his death."

"And then they killed their own man?"

"And cut his tongue out, which has all kinds of hidden meaning."

Dyatlov gave another of his little grunts, and said "Well, murder is your speciality. I just kick butt. Life is easier that way."

Pieter turned and moved around the roof space. The squad leader trailed after him.

As with the room below and the streets outside the rooftop was like a warzone. The walls and turret were blasted everywhere with burn marks and holes, and piles of debris and shell casings carpeted the floor. Opened ammo boxes, some with bullet casings or magazines still inside, lay overturned, alongside grenades and assault rifles and sun-machine guns.

Pieter stood there and looked at it, shaking his head in amazement.

"Where the hell did they get this stuff from? There's enough firepower here to equip a small army."

"My guess is that it probably came from Slovakia. That's the main route for gun smugglers these days. This kind of gear is legal over there, all you need to do is walk into a gun shop with some ID, and you can buy whatever you want. Ex-army assault rifles, C10's or C15's, anti-personnel mines, even rocket launches. It's all surplus stock from the days of the cold war. Then all they'd need to do is smuggle it back across the border into Holland. Which is pretty simple these days with open borders everywhere. Yep, if you've got the money and the motivation, it's not difficult at all my friend."

"Yeah but these guys, from my limited amount of experience, they were well trained. Getting the stuff is one thing, but knowing how to use it is another, surely?"

"True, they certainly knew what they were doing. But there are training camps all over the place. A few in the Balkans, in Scandinavia even."

This made Pieter look up. "In Finland?"

"Sure, why?"

"Just a bit of info we received with possible links to an old far-right group based there."

"Well there are thousands of places up there where they could set up a training outfit, real remote places off grid. Yeah, it would be an ideal location."

Pieter nodded.

"I could ask around if you like? I'm still in touch with some of my buddies from my days in the military. A lot of them went into private security, executive protection for dodgy politicians in the Middle East or the rich and famous in the west. It's big business these days. They might have heard of something, the odd rumour perhaps."

"Yeah I'd appreciate that. Some of them are still out there remember?" He nodded at the corpse tied to the roof turret.

Dyatlov followed his gaze. His mouth turned up like there was a bad smell. "As for that crap, the fucking witchy signs and occult nonsense, it's all mumbo jumbo to me."

CHAPTER 13

FEVER DREAMS

The rest of the afternoon and evening went by in a blur. A city-wide sweep for the escaped fugitives sprang into immediate action. The speedboat could potentially be on the far side of Amsterdam within ten minutes once it was on the main canal network. After 60 minutes it was decided to extend the search into a nation-wide manhunt, and check all border access points, and police forces across Europe were put on maximum alert.

A fierce debate began immediately within Dutch law enforcement agencies as to whether to treat this as a terrorist or domestic incident. Opinion was divided, for although on the surface it had all of the hallmarks of a terrorist attack like the Paris atrocities, the occult nature of the murder of Levi Kohnstaam led others to wonder if they were dealing with some kind of crazy cult. The symbols found on the alley wall suggested the latter.

Predictably the world's media descended on Amsterdam, with news crews from as far away as Japan and Australia clambering for exclusive updates. The media liaison department was swamped with queries, and Pieter himself had to fend off questions thrown at him by Dutch reporters gathering close to the crime scenes. It soon became a media frenzy, and photographers taking pictures from high vantage points in the surrounding buildings, using telephoto lenses, were able to capture images of Kohnstaam's body up on the roof. These pictures hit the internet within minutes, showing not just the jeweller's corpse but also the pentagram sign daubed in his own blood.

Over at the science museum the helicopter had located and retrieved the body of the youth, and his corpse, along with all of the others, was transferred to a temporary morgue. Then news had reached Pieter of another incident. There was a fire reported in Jordaan near to Rozengracht Bridge, a bakery and office premises above were engulfed in flames, and fire crews were at the scene. Eyewitnesses were talking of a malfunctioning oven in the small bakery, but Pieter suspected otherwise. It was just too much of a coincidence.

Rumours and speculation were rife all across town. The full might of the Dutch National Police Force was swinging into action.

The questions on everybody's lips were: Just who was responsible for the series of barbaric crimes and attacks? Where had they gone to ground? And when would they strike again?

One thing was clear: Whoever they were, they had announced themselves to the world in a spectacular fashion.

*   *   *

It was after midnight by the time Pieter made it back home. Lotte had left a note for him on the kitchen unit. He read her message:

Wake me when you get in. Lotte xx

It was too late to disturb her, and besides he was exhausted. Instead he quietly opened the bedroom door and looked at her sleeping form. They had gone back to their original sleeping arrangements after the first night, she in the big bedroom, and he in the smaller one. Seeing her helped to ease the worries racing around in his mind, if only temporarily. But they could talk in the morning, and so he gently closed the door again.

Passing through to the living room he briefly switched on the TV. It was still tuned to a 24hr news channel, and Pieter sat on the couch to see the latest developments, but the reporting mostly consisted of shaky footage captured on mobile phones by members of the public.

125

He watched for a while, reliving the intense firefight which the media had already christened THE BATTLE OF WEEPING TOWER. But very soon he felt his eyelids drooping, and so he put the TV on standby, kicked off his shoes and, too tired to even head to his bedroom, he lay back on the couch and was asleep within seconds.

Once again he dreamt.

As before, his dream was in monochrome, and all jerky like an old silent movie.

Stepping from bright sunlight into a dark world. With walls on either side, hemming him in tighter and tighter, he moved along the twisting passageway, deeper and deeper into the bowels of the rank underworld of the city.

The smell was appalling, making him retch. A stench like vomit and piss and animal shit. When he reached out to touch the walls he found them all sticky and slimy, and his fingertips came away smeared with something like thick mucus.

On he went, drawn inwards.

The passage was part of a huge and corrupt living thing, the walls becoming narrower but pulsing and sucking. From somewhere ahead came a dull and rhythmic thud, faint but growing louder with each step he took. A heartbeat.

Turning his head to the left and right, he saw windows that lined the walls, with the girl's faces and bodies pressed against the glass. Beckoning him inside, their lithe body's dancing seductively.

Just ahead the passageway entered a curved brick tunnel, and beyond the darkness was infinite, stretching away to nothing.

He hesitated.

Hearing a shuffling noise, bare feet scraping and sliding across the ancient cobbles underfoot.

From out of the pitch darkness emerged a naked woman, with dark hair and smoky eyes and pouted lips entrancing him with their beauty. He knew this was Mila, the girl from Estonia, and she smiled as though she recognized him too.

Unable to prevent himself, his gaze shifted downwards, over her breasts, and lower across her stomach. Yet there was no stomach, just a gaping wound, glistening like raw meat, parts of her ribs and spine showing through. From her butchered belly slithered coils of her intestines, and she held them out as though offering them to him.

From behind her stumbled a naked man. He was twitching and jitterbugging, his eyeballs bulging and their pupils shrunk to tiny pinpricks, like a person tripping on drugs. Between his legs was a bloody hole where he'd been castrated.

After him came his father, hunched over on spindly legs, a twisted and stooped old man with a wasted face. His bare skin was starting to corrupt to a sickly grey and green colour, and parts of his flesh had been eaten away, nibbled by tiny creatures. In his wake he left damp footprints on the ground.

Finally the fat jeweller, his huge and bloated body rippling and trembling, with his arms outstretched as he groped around like a blind man, for his eyes had been gouged out. He tried to speak, but all that came out of his mouth was a quiet mewling noise.

They came out of the shadows, their hands reaching forward to grab him, their cold, dead fingers probing his face and mouth and eyes.

Pulling him back into the dank tunnel.

Pieter awoke with a loud yell, twisting and thrashing and pushing the hands away.

He sat bolt upright and looked around at his surroundings, and then remembered falling asleep on the couch. The living room light was still on, and the wall clock told him it was the very early hours of the morning.

Slowly his heartbeat came back to normal and he sat forward and rubbed at his face, his eyes blinking away the residual images of the dream.

He heard the door opening behind him and he turned to see Lotte standing there with a concerned frown on her face. She moved towards the couch and placed her hand gently on his back.

"I heard you shouting."

"Sorry," he mumbled sleepily.

"Bad dream?"

"You could say that."

She gave his shoulder a comforting squeeze and came around to the front. "Budge up."

Pieter shifted across and she squashed in next to him, the hem of her nightie rising over her thighs. She pressed against him and hugged him tightly.

"It's been a long day for you."

"The longest of my life," he corrected with the faintest of smiles. "A tough few days in fact."

"I waited up. I didn't want to text you, thought you'd be swamped with work, but you should have woke me when you got back." She took a hold of his hand and splayed her fingers between his, squeezing them affectionately. "But never mind."

Pieter wrapped his other arm around her and held her tightly, and his body gave a huge shiver as the tension came out. Then he stretched his legs out, the last dregs from the bad dream slowly evaporating from memory.

"I heard about everything on my way over, and then spent most of the evening watching the news. Was kinda hoping to catch a glimpse of you, maybe the big hero being interviewed, having your fifteen minutes."

"Well it wasn't quite like that. To be honest, everything is such a whirl that my head's still spinning. I think I mostly acted on instinct…and training."

Lotte looked up at him earnestly, her big eyes roving over his face, and that worried frown back on her brow. "Tell me what happened."

Pieter told her everything. From his and Daan Beumers meeting with Levi Kohnstaam earlier in the day, the phone call from Beumers telling him about tailing their suspect to Schreierstoren Tower, his panicked drive over and hoping to catch his colleague before he did anything rash. The fierce gun battle that had developed, followed by him chasing one of the gunmen, and the youth's shocking leap to his death. Then later seeing his dead friend. He explained a little about the massive manhunt currently underway, how the whole country was on high alert. He finished by telling her that the investigation was massively complex and there was no end in sight just yet.

Lotte listened attentively, without asking any questions, happy to let him talk and get things out of his system. When he was done, she prodded him in the stomach.

"You know, you can't do everything yourself. You should let some of the others shoulder some of the responsibility. You already have enough on your plate with your father, they'll understand if you wanted to step back. You're going to suffer from burn out if you are not careful."

"But it's my case. I want to see this through to the end. Get the bastards responsible."

"Okay," she replied quietly. A hush descended for a moment, a nice lull that felt good. Then she whispered: "I want to help you."

Pieter looked at her upturned face, an unspoken question on his lips.

"I can do something, to help with the strain you're under."

Then she placed her hand over the front of his trousers and gently squeezed him.

"Please let me."

Pieter squirmed, partly from awkwardness but mostly from the shiver her touch sent through him. "Lotte, I'm not sure."

"It will be good for you. And for me. We both need the release."

"You're a lovely girl, but ah, it feels-"

"It feels right." She placed a finger over his lips, nuzzled his neck. "No more talking."

She unfastened his trousers and took him in her hand, squeezing and flexing until he was hard, and Pieter, his breathing coming faster, felt his passion rising. Taking a hold of his hand she glided it up under the hem of her nightie, where he felt her moistness, and her legs parted for him.

She undressed him, using her fingers and mouth on his body, and he now felt shivers of desire pass through him in waves, so he grabbed her and pulled her nightclothes away, nearly ripping the material, and she gave a small squeak of delight as he pushed her down onto the couch, and so she parted her legs even more but he pushed them wider still and thrust himself deeply inside. She was breathing hard like him, and thrusting up, as he drove his pelvis down, her breasts flushed and aroused, and she shivered as he finished inside her, calling out his name as he thrust one final time.

He gazed down, but now her eyes were pure black orbs, and her mouth stretched wide, impossibly so, until her jaw was distended, and she bit his neck as her passion continued, and her hand closed around his throat and squeezed.

A deep snicker came from her lips. Pieter flung her away in panic.

Again Pieter awoke with a shout, beating at the air to fend her off, and rolled off the couch onto the floor. He jumped to his feet, aware in the back of his mind that he was fully clothed, and he saw that the room was empty.

"Fuck!" he shouted, as the dream flickered in his mind before fading completely.

*   *   *

Sometime during the night while he had been sleeping Lotte had quietly left, taking her few possessions with her. She left no message or forwarding address, and when he tried her number there was no connection, no voicemail recording, just silence. Without a word, she had gone.

GRISSLEHAMNS – UPPSALA DISTRICT – SWEDEN. MARCH 1946.

After leaving the Convent of The Sisters of the Precious Blood, the two of them, Wenzel and Agent Gerdi, the young novice nun, had struck north. Driving in a stolen farm vehicle and using forged papers, they made good progress. Europe was just getting back to its feet after years of war but passage was much easier now, as long as they did not draw unnecessary attention. If anybody stopped them, then they were brother and younger sister trying to reach their home to be reunited with family, just like the millions of other displaced citizens.

After two weeks they passed over the Kiel Canal and then crossed the border into Denmark. Wenzel had planned this escape route many months before. Taking Gerdi with him hadn't been part of it originally, but he realized that one young man travelling alone would still attract unwanted attention, and she had been of huge help, so allowing her to accompany him and thus avoid detection herself would be an advantage for them both. But with the onset of winter their journey had slowed to a crawl, and he decided they should see out the worst of the snows and bed down in a safe house in Copenhagen.

With the arrival of spring their journey had resumed. Crossing over into neighbouring Sweden at Malmö, they had headed north-east. Wishing to avoid the capital of Stockholm Wenzel instead drove into Uppsala, a wild and rugged district with a craggy coastline overlooking the cold waters of the Gulf of Bothnia. Finally in late March they had arrived at the tiny fishing hamlet of Grisslehamns, and awaited passage on board the fishing vessel MFV Toró, bound for the islands of Åland and their final destination – Finland.

They spent the time waiting by booking into a small ramshackle boarding house, offering to pay double as long as the elderly proprietor did not pry into their business. Happy to take the money, he left them be, and Wenzel and the girl whiled away the time by sitting on the porch and enjoying the stiff breeze blowing in.

Wenzel at times recalled events back at the convent.

Killing Mother Annette and the other nuns had been an abhorrent but unavoidable evil. Their screams and pleas for mercy, echoing around inside the stone walls, were pitiful and harrowing to hear, but Wenzel was ruthless, and carried out the task with the help of the novice nun without hesitation. Together they had chased them down one by one, their knives ripping and cutting and plunging at them in a sick orgy of bloodlust.

When it was done they returned to the small room hidden deep beneath the convent where the sleeping babes lay in their cribs. Retrieving his knapsack from the floor Wenzel had removed a number of other items. First a pair of large syringes, one of which he handed to Gerdi. Then the glass phial given to him by the beautiful She-Wolf Ilse Hirsch as she had lain wounded in the grass, with its contents of blood and semen.

Placing it on a small shelf, he and the girl had moved from crib to crib, quietly and gently drawing blood from the tiny infants. Most had slept through with barely a flicker, or at most a little murmur, before resuming the sleep of the innocents, unharmed and unaware.

Finished with this task, Wenzel had removed the stopper from the glass phial and they had emptied the contents of their syringes into the mixture, the potent combination of sweet blood and male seed and menstrual energy creating a powerful unifying force.

And finally, Wenzel and the girl had used salt to lay down the necessary symbols on the stone floor, the markings and letters and pentagrams, copied from the heavy leather-bound file called UNTERNEHMEN WERWOLF that Wenzel had read back at Hulchrath Castle over a year and a half ago. Those strange and otherworldly signs, together with the obscure rituals and the incantations he now spoke, his voice echoing in the dark room beneath the convent.

On the evening of their second day of waiting, they received word that the fishing trawler would be leaving on the morning tide. They were to be ready, with any baggage they required, on the small stone pier at first light.

Later that night Wenzel drove their farmer's truck further up the coast and left it amidst the sand dunes, then walked back to the boarding house.

They slept a little. Yet the anticipation of what was to be the final leg of his long journey, and the prospect of reaching a safe haven, meant he could not rest for long. So in the early hours the two of them made their way down the grassy slope from the boarding house, each carrying a small suitcase, Wenzel still wearing the knapsack with its priceless items inside.

The MFV Toró was waiting for them. It was a sturdy-looking wooden vessel, normally crewed by three or four men, but for this trip Wenzel had insisted on just the captain. He was being paid handsomely and so was happy to oblige.

Climbing on board, they both immediately went below deck.

A few minutes later the boat set out across the water, heading east into the brightening dawn sky.

The world was to hear no more of Herbert Wenzel.

CHAPTER 14

PRISHA KAPOOR, AND THE FOOT-TRACK SPELL

He had no time to think about Lotte's whereabouts, for his mobile phone immediately started to jangle and buzz with notifications of updates and messages from work.

General requests for information and answers to a multitude of queries had built up overnight, including questions from the media who had somehow got a hold of his number. These latter he ignored. Pieter scrolled through the others, picking out one or two of the more important ones, and did his best to respond, either by phone call or email. The others could wait until he arrived at HQ.

This took up an hour. He managed to snatch a quick breakfast, and then he dashed down the stairs and out the front door, where his driver was waiting for him. His own car, damaged in the shootout, was in the compound, and he would pick up a temporary replacement from the carpool later.

His first stop was the hospital morgue. He'd received a garbled voicemail message from the Chief Pathologist, Prisha Kapoor, which sounded quite urgent.

Overnight all of the bodies had been ferried over from the temporary morgue to the hospital. When he strode through the automatic doors, Pieter was confronted with the gruesome sight of several rows of corpses lined up on autopsy tables awaiting examination, with still more stored away in the freezer storage units.

Some of the bodies were still bagged up, whereas others were laid out, unclothed and being processed. Prisha and one of her assistants were busy at work. To say they were snowed under was an understatement.

At the moment she was gowned and masked up and using a small circular saw to cut away the top portion of a man's skull. The high-pitched noise set Pieter's teeth on edge, and a fine white mist sprayed up as she worked.

He watched from the other side of the room, feeling like a morbid ghoul, fascinated and repulsed in equal measures. Prisha prized away the skull section and placed it to one side, and then reached into the cavity and, with a loud sucking noise, pulled the brain free and plopped it into a set of scales. Her assistant, a pale-faced young man with bug-out eyes, made notes on his iPad.

Prisha glanced up then and noticed him. Saying something to her assistant, she removed her plastic face-shield and waddled over to the wash basins. Snapping off her latex gloves and binning them, she washed her hands and arms, and then joined him.

"I was on my annual leave until this happened," she told him grumpily, as though blaming him personally. "I've been here since midnight."

"Sorry."

Prisha looked him up and down sternly, then her features softened a little. "From what I hear, you're lucky not to be one of my specimens today."

"Hope you're not disappointed?"

"You're a man. By default you're all a disappointment."

"But aren't you gay?"

"Yes," she fixed him with her stare, "and now you know why." Spinning on her heels she beckoned over her shoulder. "Follow me."

She gave him a tour around the room, leading him up and down the rows of cadavers.

"As you would guess, most of the victims from yesterday's attack died from gunshot wounds or shrapnel wounds resulting in severe trauma and blood loss. There are a few exceptions. Your colleague, Mr Beumers, died from asphyxiation. The overweight man over there," she pointed at the obese naked form of Levi Kohnstamm, "he suffered a massive coronary, so wasn't technically murdered. The eyes and tongue were removed post mortem. And the one who jumped from the roof of the science museum, he experienced multiple blunt fractures from impacting the water, and then drowned. He's bagged up over there."

Pieter noted the short row of bodies still in their body bags were slightly separate from the rest.

Prisha stopped before another one of the victims. The figure on the metal autopsy table was burnt beyond all recognition, and he had adopted the familiar pugilistic attitude of most burn victims, a 'boxer-like' body posture of flexed arms and knees and clenched fists. The smell was revolting, and Pieter took an involuntary step backwards.

"This was the tram driver. When we found him he was still in his seat at the front of the tram, hunched over his controls."

After a moment, she resumed her stroll.

"All very normal from a pathological point of view. Normal, that is, until we come to these." She came to a halt next to the row of body bags.

There were six of them lined up against the back wall.

"The attackers I'm guessing?"

"Correct. Again, most of them died from injuries sustained during the battle. Nothing odd about that. I didn't pay much attention to them initially. I wanted to start with their victims, the members of the public and the police officers, and so most of last night and through the early hours I concentrated on the other deceased. It was only when I checked on them a short time ago that I noticed... ah..."

Pieter glanced at her. "Noticed what?"

Prisha pursed her lips, her eyes darting back and forth over his face as though weighing something up in her mind.

"Perhaps you'd better see for yourself."

She reached across and slowly unzipped the nearest body bag, and then stood back to watch his reaction.

Pieter didn't know how to react. He didn't fully comprehend at first what he was actually seeing.

Inside was the skeletal remains of one of the gunmen. Not a fresh corpse as he was expecting, but just bones. A full set, laid out on the table, the bones already turning brown with age. Some of them actually rotting and crumbling, with the skull having already collapsed in on itself.

"These are not the bones of a recently deceased person, Inspector. I've worked on several cases involving the discovery of interred murder victims, many of them dug up decades after they died. So I know old bones when I see them. I will need to do more tests to be sure, but I'd estimate that if I didn't know otherwise this person, and the other five with him, died many years ago."

As if to prove her point she reached out and touched the rib cage with the tip of her pen, and the bone crumbled to dust.

Pieter had no response. The skeleton on the table, along with all of the other cadavers set out in the room or stored away in the freezer unit, was no more than eighteen hours old. But the level of decomposition overnight to these six was undeniably much more advanced than that, was of the nature of someone long-dead. The flesh and organs had already gone, a process that would takes months if not years, until all that remained was a pile of old bones turning to dust.

He became aware that Prisha was looking at him. Perhaps she was not expecting a reply from him. Going from the expression on her face, a worried frown creasing her brow and a hint of fear in her eyes, she merely wanted confirmation that he saw what she saw. That she wasn't imaging this.

Eventually she broke the silence herself.

"If you think that is weird, then wait for this."

She walked away and then came back with a sheet of paper. Catching a brief glimpse he saw a list of letters and notations, lots of medical words that made little sense to him.

"The results of the tests on your soil sample. I was told that you found this in your home?" She appeared sceptical.

"That's right. On the floor of my attic."

"Right. Well, they ran various tests to determine what it was, what compounds and chemicals it was made up of. So I can tell you that it contains, amongst other things, oxygen bacteria of the Enterobacteriaceae family such as gram-positive cocci and Stayhylococcus. They then heated the sample to detect traces of yeasts and mould, as well as – get this – saline fungi."

Prisha, seeing the confused and slightly glazed look on his face, lowered the paper she'd been reading from.

"I'll put it more simply for you. The soil from your house contains seaweed and soil from a cemetery. Grave dirt."

Pieter gave a nervous little laugh. "Ok"

"Can I tell you something? And you must promise me that this goes no further than these four walls." She'd lowered her voice, but her assistant was well out of earshot. "I have my reputation to maintain."

"Knock yourself out."

"My partner, Rowan, she is into all kinds of whacky stuff. New age remedies, Wiccan legends, Harry Potter. It must come from her Irish roots. Anyway, during our time together I have picked up the odd piece of trivia from her regarding these things, she leaves books lying around the flat which when I'm bored I have glanced through, like you do."

Pieter nodded encouragement, wondering where this was going.

"Have you heard of a foot-track spell?"

"Pardon? A what?"

"A foot-track spell. Somebody who wishes you harm will put a concoction of ingredients, such as elements from animal foetuses, baby blood, soil from the grave of a recently deceased person, really revolting things like that, they will put this on the floor where a person – in this case you - will walk through it. To curse them, to cross them. Did you walk through it?"

Pieter looked at her, his mouth hanging open, wondering if she'd been on the weed overnight.

"Uh… yes, I think so."

"Do you have the shoes or slippers you were wearing?"

"I was in my bare feet."

"Shit, then you have a problem."

"I do?"

"Well if you believe this kind of thing," Prisha smiled at him sheepishly. "Which, being of a scientific bent, I don't. But if you were susceptible to it, and open-minded enough to be concerned, then certain consequences may occur as a result of walking through a foot-track spell."

"Consequences?"

"Of a health-related nature. Things like heart attacks, strokes, dementia, or death. Have you been feeling unwell lately? Or perhaps depressed?"

Pieter shrugged. "I'm fit as a fiddle. No coughs or sneezes. My digital prostrate check came back all good."

"Well, it's all to do with the power of suggestion of course. Spells and curses. It's not the fact that you may or may not have had a curse put on you, but whether you believe it or not. If you firmly believe that you have been crossed, then that in itself is enough for you to talk yourself into feeling unwell, convinced that every ache and pain is a sign that you have some fatal illness."

"And me being a cynical, world-weary, non-believing copper rules that out?"

"Naturally." Prisha handed him the sheet of paper, trying to smile but still looking frazzled and nervous. "Nothing for you to worry about then."

As he left, Pieter wondered why he'd failed to mention the vivid and terrifying nightmares haunting him at night.

Pieter climbed back into the car and told his driver to head over to HQ. But the driver, a bald cop called Joos, shook his head.

"Another lead's come in, sir. A witness."

*   *   *

Amstelsluizen was a series of huge locks on the river Amstel. It comprised of five massive concrete sluice gates, each about 75 metres long, running parallel with the river. Every twelve hours, the sluice gates were opened, allowing a flow of fresh water to pour into Amsterdam's canal system from the eastern side of the city, whilst over on the west a similar set of locks allowed the old water to gush out. It was supposed to ensure that the water in the canals was constantly fresh and clean enough to drink – or so they claimed. It worked as regular as clockwork, so much so that the average Amsterdammer never even noticed it was happening.

Joos pulled up in the parking area near the riverside, and Pieter climbed out. He stood for a moment, enjoying the relative quiet in this part of the city, away from the hustle and bustle of the centre. A few gulls swooped down onto the broad river, and further upstream was the distinctive shape of Skinny Bridge.

He breathed in a couple of lungful's of unpolluted air, and then leaned back into the open window.

"Are you carrying your gun Joos?" His own was still at work, left there overnight.

"Sure am sir. New orders, every officer is to be armed as from today. Even the traffic cops are carrying their side arms again."

"Ok, well keep an eye out will you? But hang back a little. If this witness is a crusty old sea dog type he might be more inclined to talk more if I see him alone."

"Locked and loaded sir." Joos patted the holster on his waist belt.

The lock-keeper in charge of the sluice gates was way past retirement age, Pieter estimated. But considering his main task was to press a button that operated the gates just twice a day, the job probably wasn't too taxing.

Pieter found him sitting in a deck chair just outside the main control building – actually a small tin Quonset hut. He was wearing a life vest and had a pair of wireless headphones clamped on his head, and even though it was not yet eleven in the morning he already had a bottle of Bud Lite in his hand. He did not hear Pieter approach, and when he tapped him on the shoulder, the old guy nearly levitated out of his chair. He belatedly tried to hide his beer, and then thought, what was the point?

"What the heck you doing, sneaking up on me like that?" He talked loud, because of the headphones. "Coulda' shit my pants."

Pieter flashed his badge, which set off another futile attempt to slide the beer out of sight.

"You not gonna breathalyse me are you? I got no puff, not with these clapped out old lungs."

"The sun's just about over the yardarm, so I think you're allowed." Pieter moved over to the railing alongside the hut and leaned back. "I understand you gave us a call? That you may have seen something important, in relation to the attack."

"Aye, that's right. I called last night. You guys took your time."

"Well I'm here now, so why don't you tell me?"

The lock-keeper, feeling more relaxed, took a swig from his beer and then removed the headphones. "It was the hooligans. In the boat. Damn ruffians."

Pieter smiled his friendly smile, which encouraged the old man to explain further.

"They came right along the river at full speed. Straight under Skinny Bridge over there, and then right through the locks, without slowing. Not only is it illegal to break the speed limit, but anybody passing through the locks has to get permission. From me. I have to carefully note all of the vessels that pass through, who they are registered to, and if anybody disobeys then they are apt to have their boat seized. I take my job very seriously you know." He took another sip.

Pieter looked back over his shoulder at Skinny Bridge and the city skyline beyond, the direction from which this boat came from. "What kind of boat was it?"

"A speed boat! And it was moving like they were in a real big hurry. Bugging out, I think they call it." The lock-keeper seemed to be enjoying himself now, loving being the centre of attention. "I thought at first they were shooting another one of those James Bond movies or something. Was going to see if I could get Daniel Craig's autograph.

But then they swerved in to the side, and everybody on board jumped onto that small concrete jetty down there and rushed up the staircase."

He was pointing to a tiny landing tucked into the high side of the river, just a little further upstream.

"They didn't tie it up, just leaped out. And they were armed. I could see that clearly, they had rifles and big guns."

"How many were there?"

"Three or four. I didn't do a head count, because those stairs come right past this spot, and I ducked inside my hut. Anyways, they didn't see me, which considering what they done over at the tower yesterday tells me I was damn lucky they didn't, otherwise they'd have stopped to finish me off. If it was the same people that is. Do you think it was the same people mister?"

"It certainly sounds like it. What happened to the boat?"

"It floated away some, but not far. It got caught up in that bunch of trees over there, where the wall juts out. You can still see it."

Pieter certainly could. It was bumping and rocking gently in the water, but didn't look to be going anywhere anytime soon.

"What did they do next? Once they reached the top of the stairs?"

"There was a black van waiting for them at the roadside. It had blacked out windows, and had its engine running, like the occupants were ready for a quick getaway, and they all got into the back and off it sped. There must have been someone in the back because the rear doors were flung open from the inside."

The old lock-keeper came to his feet then, his knees creaking like pieces of river flotsam. He walked to the edge of the lock where a short gangplank joined it to the pathway running along the riverside. He pointed towards the long street leading away from the river.

"They drove hell for leather down Utrechtstraat and then turned right at the end."

Pieter joined him, noting that a turn to the right would have taken them over Prinsengracht canal. Back toward the city centre.

Pieter and Joos clambered down to the muddy riverbank and pushed their way through the trees to the spot where the speedboat had drifted ashore. The front had become fouled up in some old discarded pallets and they had to shift these to one side and then pull the boat further up the banking.

"You'll have to get the stern and push it. We don't want it floating away on the high tide."

"Thanks," Joos replied, and waded out into the water.

Together they managed to get it onto the riverbank beneath the trees. Grabbing a rope that was dangling over the side, Joos tied it to a tree trunk and then stood back, wiping the mud off his hands and looking at his ruined shoes and trousers.

Pieter clambered aboard to have a quick and cursory look around. However, he soon established there wasn't much of note, just a pair of gloves on the pilot's leather seat up front. There were no discarded firearms. But the keys were still in the ignition.

Jumping back down he said to Joos: "You'd better call it in, get somebody to tow it away to the forensics shop. Then you can drop me off somewhere else for a few minutes, before giving me a ride back to HQ."

"Anything you say, sir."

*   *   *

He decided it was time to pay Bart another visit over at The Newcastle Bar.

As the morning wore on he had become increasingly concerned for Lotte's wellbeing, puzzled over her sudden departure, and more than a little worried over her safety and whereabouts. He had tried calling again, and texted her, but to no avail, and by lunchtime a small knot of tension had started to form in his stomach.

Loos dropped him off around the corner. Pieter told him to wait in the car again.

The bar itself was still shut, but the large doors were open and a delivery driver was busy lugging in crates and barrels of beer for the lunchtime trade. Pieter strolled in and looked around for Bart.

He was just coming up from the beer cellar, huffing and puffing as he emerged through the trapdoor behind the bar.

As his head appeared from out of the hole he made eye contact with Pieter, and a flicker of alarm crossed the barman's face, before it morphed into a look of fear. He froze in place, his lower body out of sight, but then he dropped his hands back down into the opening, and Pieter wondered if he was reaching for a weapon, a baseball bat perhaps. But then Bart slowly climbed out through the trapdoor, unarmed, and stood there looking meek and unthreatening.

"What do you want?" he mumbled. Pieter saw his face was still swollen with bruises.

"Have you seen Lotte recently? Or spoken to her?"

"What? No! Not since she left." He was standing well back from the bar, as though worried that Pieter might vault over and start punching him again, which he was tempted to do.

"Are you sure? You better not be lying to me. If I find out you are, and you've threatened her again or hurt her." He left the consequences of that to Bart's imagination.

But the fat barman was shaking his head, and looking petrified. "I want nothing more to do with that bitch. I'm glad to see the back of her. Why?"

Pieter just told him: "it's none of your business why."

But then a light seemed to come on in Bart's head, a rare moment of intelligence, as he put two and two together. "Ha, she's left you already. Your girlfriend's dumped you. Hasn't she?"

He suddenly looked emboldened, which pissed Pieter off, and so he took two quick strides towards the bar, and Bart shrunk away in terror. He stared hard into the barman's face, and then turned and walked out.

CHAPTER 15

THE HOSPITAL MORGUE

After Pieter left, Prisha Kapoor processed one more body in the hospital morgue and then instructed her assistant to clean up and store away the bodies inside the freezer units. Except for the body bags containing the bones: he was to leave those for the time being. Then she went to get some rest.

Her office was at the end of the corridor. She contemplated switching on her computer and typing up some reports, as there was a huge backlog of paperwork to be finished. But she was too exhausted, and perturbed by the day's events. Instead she crossed to the small cot made up in the corner of the room and lowered herself onto the thin mattress with a sigh.

Sitting there with her hands covering her face, she gently massaged at the dull ache building up behind her eyes, hoping it was just a tension headache and not the first signs of a migraine.

Back in the main room her assistant was just finishing cleaning up the dissecting equipment and replacing them into their correct drawers and racks.

Into one tray went the abdominal scissors and the bone shears and the spinal column saw, while on the wall hooks went the bone mallet and the post-mortem hammer and the skull breaker. All cleaned with disinfectant solution and now spotless. Then he plugged in the small hand-held 120V autopsy saw which needed recharging, before turning to the bone sectional saw – his favourite piece of equipment.

This was essentially the same as the meat-slicers found in most butcher's shops, but the cutting blades had tiny high-powered water jets that enabled them to cut straight through thick bone, slicing off very thin slivers. It was a very neat tool, and was ridiculously expensive, but boy was it a pain to clean up. Every tiny scrap of flesh and bone and meat had to be picked out by hand and by brush, as even the most microscopic sliver of flesh could get stuck in the saw's blades and foul it up. Nevertheless it needed to be done and the young assistant went about the task with meticulous care.

When he was done he switched the machine on and turned it up to full speed, enjoying the gentle hum and buzz and watching the sharp steel blades spin around in a blur just inches from his hand. Satisfied that it was all in good working order, he switched off and carried it across to the storage unit.

It was as he was bending over and sliding it into place that he heard a noise. A rattling sound, coming from behind him.

Still hunched over he turned his head to look back over his shoulder, but there was nothing amiss. Nothing had fallen over or rolled onto the floor, everything was just as it should be. He turned back and locked the cupboard door, then straightened up. There was just one more job and then he was done.

He wheeled the autopsy table across to the freezer units against the far wall, and flipped over the elevation surface, and tucked it up against the wall, all stored away neat and tidy.

The sound came again, louder this time. Definitely something rattling, like a clinking noise, and something sliding as well. What the heck was it? He stood there and looked around the room, trying to pinpoint its source.

Then, out of the corner of his eye, he caught a movement in his peripheral vison and turned to look. Lined up against the wall on their gurneys were the body bags containing the remains of the gunmen killed yesterday, zipped up and awaiting further tests. But as he looked, one of them moved slightly.

He stared, thinking he was seeing things. Then it happened again, the bad moving and flexing and part of it bulging outwards, and there was that damn queer rattling noise again, coming from inside the bag.

Unable to tear his eyes away, and so petrified at what was happening that he remained frozen and rooted to the spot, he watched as slowly the zipper was pushed down from the inside, the metal fastener sliding further and further.

It paused briefly, and then a long, narrow bony finger poked out of the small gap and continued pushing the zipper, opening the body bag wider and wider.

The blood-curdling scream jolted Prisha's already shaky heart, sending a spasm of dread through her entire body.

She came to her feet so fast that she stumbled and nearly lost her balance. Then she grabbed the door handle and rushed out into the corridor.

The lights were off. She didn't remember turning them off, but she saw that the main room where the bodies were kept was in darkness too, so she assumed her assistant had finished his tasks and gone home.

Yet if that was the case then who was it she'd heard screaming?

As she thought this there was more commotion, the sound of smashing and banging, coming down the corridor, as though there was a struggle going on. Prisha hurried forward.

Throwing open the plastic swing doors of the morgue, she reached out and flicked on the bank of light switches on the wall, and the darkness in the room flickered to white as the fluorescent bulbs stuttered into life.

In that half-second, as the blackness and whiteness flashed back and forth, she saw something that stopped her breath. A terrifying sight that was instantly ingrained on her brain.

A figure, standing there and looking at her. All twisted and out of shape. Made of bones.

It was deformed, as though some of the bones were in the wrong place or not there at all. Some of the ribcage was gone, as was one of the lower arm bones. The spine was all disjointed and twisted to the side like someone with a terrible back injury, and the skull was tilted sideways. Worse of all was the jaw, which had slipped down so it looked all lopsided, like someone who had been punched by a boxer.

Prisha stood totally still as the flickering boneman shambled towards her.

"So what happened then?" Pieter asked, dreading hearing her answer.

"Nothing. The lights came on, and the figure was gone. Whoever, or rather *whatever,* it was had disappeared. It was only there for a split-second, and then the next instant it wasn't."

She pointed across the room. "All that was here was that pile of bones over on the floor ."

Prisha seemed to visibly sag just then and she grabbed a stool and dragged it across, sitting down before she fell down.

"And your assistant?"

"I couldn't see him. I thought he wasn't around. Was quickly trying to tell myself that I'd imagined the whole thing, that I was overworked and tired. But then I heard him crying very faintly."

Pieter stood quietly, waiting patiently for her to explain events in her own time.

"He was hiding inside one of the freezer units. There was a body in there with him, one of the gun attack victims, but he'd managed somehow to squeeze himself in there with it. The boy was so petrified that he decided it was preferable to hide in there rather than stay out here. Can you imagine that? He saw something so frightening that he chose to do that?"

Pieter couldn't.

"If he saw that thing, in here." Prisha's chin started to tremble. She was on the verge of tears, and so she sucked in a big lungful of air in an attempt to steady her own fractured nerves.

When Pieter had arrived about ten minutes ago there had been total pandemonium in this part of the hospital. Doctors and medics were dashing here and there, and people were shouting and screaming hysterically.

He'd pushed his way through the crowd in time to see Prisha been comforted by her colleagues, with tears streaming down her face, pointing back towards the morgue behind her, mouthing something incoherent about bones and hands reaching for her. Pieter had squeezed himself into the morgue itself. Inside a pair of burly porters were attempting to restrain the young lab assistant, who was on the floor thrashing and kicking and biting at them, screaming himself hoarse. Eventually they had managed to drag him away, but only after a doctor had injected him with a sedative.

After they had left, Pieter had stood there and looked around, seeing the opened freezer unit with the body still laid inside, and the pile of old bones on the floor alongside the row of gurneys. There were five body bags still there, with the remains still neatly tagged and zipped up inside, and one opened bag draped half on the floor.

Now, listening to Prisha describe what had happened, he asked himself yet again: what the hell was going on?

CHAPTER 16

THE FINLAND OCCULT CONNECTION

Having earlier picked up a replacement car from the police car pool on Elandsgracht, Pieter drove himself back to HQ. Walking into his corner office, he was surprised to find Dyatlov and Floris de Kok waiting for him. Cluttering up much of the floor space were five or six large box files, some with their contents spilled out across the carpet. Adolf was on his hands and knees going through them methodically. Dyatlov had appropriated his desk and chair, where he had his own laptop opened out, the screen filled with writing.

"Have I been fired?" Pieter asked, looking at the mess.

"Sorry about this Van Dijk. It looks worse than it is, but Adolf here tells me he has everything in order."

"We hear there was some weird things happening over at the hospital?" Floris asked in a somewhat excited state.

"There isn't a suitable word to describe it. Bizarre, odd, inexplicable, take your pick."

Floris waited for him to go on, but Pieter wouldn't have known where to begin had he been inclined to fill them in on events, which he wasn't. Instead he asked, "So what's going on?"

"Better close the door," Dyatlov told him. "And grab yourself a seat"

Pieter borrowed one from the squad room and rolled it through his doorway, closed the door, and sat down with the seat backed up against the door to keep it shut.

"Ok, you told me yesterday about some possible links to Scandinavia, particularly Finland. I said I'd ask some of my old contacts if they'd heard anything on the grapevine. Adolf told me about the signet rings and also the message on the wall near the first murder scene." He held up a photo showing the Werewolf warning and symbol.

"That's right. Interpol came back with a matching symbol connected to a series of murders there in the 1970's. Far Right stuff."

"Yes, Adolf here has pulled the files on those killings, and our friends in Helsinki have sent through everything they had at their end. They seemed surprised we were looking into that case, because as far as they are concerned it's old news, the case solved and closed years ago. Which admittedly, going off the amount of info here they did a pretty thorough job, and caught the killers. No dispute there."

"But there are links to our case?"

"Indirectly. Only in the sense that they were carried out by people of the same neo-Nazi persuasion. And ever since the Anders Breivik mass killings in Norway, our Scandinavian friends have really set to work sweeping up all of the skin-head Hitler fanatics, and cracking down on their activities. So as far as any current quasi-paramilitary training camps go, I'm afraid I've drawn a blank."

He saw the look of disappointment on Pieter's face, and quickly added, "But my guys are still checking that out. So something might turn up on that score. But listen, the murders themselves, you need to hear the details about them."

He held out his hand to Adolf who passed up a thick cardboard file. "Everything was filed by hand on paper back then. We're talking about the late 1970's and the early 1980's, before digitization. So it's a long process going through it all, and I'm only about half way through the stuff. But it's quite amazing the amount of work detectives did, the interviews, the door-to-door enquiries, vehicle registration checks, which they all wrote into their reports and put into their forms.

It puts us modern cops to shame." Adolf bent over and went back to work, thumbing his way through another large box.

Dyatlov took up the story again. "It's not entirely clear when the murders first began. Throughout the 1970's, like elsewhere in Europe, various far-right groups sprang up in Finland, and with them the number of racial attacks increased. These were reasonably low-key affairs initially, black or Asian kids being jumped in the street and beat up, racial slurs, the usual kind of thing. Then, in 1978, a new group popped up, a Hell's Angels type group who started to make their presence felt by upping the ante."

He leafed through several pages and then continued. "The first confirmed murder attributed to this group was in August 1978. An Asian shopkeeper was set upon by a number of men wearing leather jackets and motorbike helmets. He was beaten up with baseball bats and left on the floor of his shop. The place was ransacked but no money was stolen from the till. On the wall outside was sprayed a symbol – similar, but not identical, to the one near our first crime scene. The shopkeeper was in a coma for three days, after which he died. The Finnish police assumed that it was a racially-motivated beating that went just a bit too far."

He passed a sheet of paper to Pieter. It was an old autopsy report, but in Finnish. Attached to it with paperclips were two colour crime-scene photographs. One showed the interior of the shop: all of the shelves had been turned over with their produce scattered across the shop aisles, and on the floor was a large pool of blood where the victim had been left. The second photograph was of the symbol spray-painted beside the entranceway.

"The second confirmed murder – they know it was definitely the same bunch of killers because again they left their calling card behind, the symbol – this one happened the following spring. On a quiet forest road about fifty miles northwest of Helsinki, an Asian driver was pulled from his car. His vehicle was set on fire, and the man was chained to the back of one of the motorbikes and dragged along behind it for several miles. Then he was stabbed over two hundred times. The blood spray patterns showed that he was still alive at the time. He also put up a hell of a fight, as he tried dragging himself along the roadway even whilst they were repeatedly stabbing him. The victim left a wife and three daughters.

More murders followed throughout the year. An Imam had his house firebombed while he and his wife slept upstairs. They both died.

Two black girls, aged fifteen and sixteen, were gang-raped, tied to a tree and bludgeoned with house bricks. This happened during the daytime in a park in central Helsinki. Nobody came forward with witness statements.

And so on. The details are all here in the file, most of it had been translated into Dutch so you can go through it later."

Dyatlov paused, and Floris glanced up. "That's when things started to change, and get even weirder as well. Tell him."

"He's right. Up to then it seemed that the Finnish police were dealing with an extreme right-wing bunch of Nazi fanatics. All of their victims fit the type to suggest this. But in late 1979 to early 1980, they broadened their attacks to include white people, both male and female. A young female teacher killed in her home – it turned out that she had a black boyfriend, so it was thought she may have been targeted for having what was referred to back then as an interracial relationship. Yet this was followed by three white factory workers gunned down in the street after finishing their shift. A white boy, aged two, snatched from his mother's arms and thrown off a bridge into a river by a group of passing motorbike riders. And all connected, either by the symbol or the presence of this group of Hell's Angels. Yet now, for the first time, the crimes were no longer been treated as racist attacks."

"That would fit with our murders here," Pieter interjected. "None of our victims fit one particular ethnicity group or age. A prostitute from East Europe possibly, that may have riled them, but none of the others anyway."

Dyatlov nodded enthusiastically. "It turned out the cops in Helsinki were right. Fairly soon after, pretty much by chance in fact, they made a number of arrests, and their real motive," he shook his head here in an expression of disbelief, "their real motive became clear."

"They got lucky? Or they made a breakthrough?"

"Definitely the former. The drugs squad carried out a series of raids across the country, breaking up dealers supply chains and busting cannabis farms. One of these raids took place in a disused warehouse on Drumsö Island – back then this was part of the run-down docks, before the Yuppies moved in and turned it into a trendy yachting marina. Well, they smashed the doors down and took the people inside completely by surprise, but what they found in there wasn't an illegal drugs operation but what the police described as a torture chamber. A group of bikers – yep, the exact same ones – had a guy strapped to a workbench and were sawing off his arms and legs. Nearby was a bucket filled with other amputated limbs from other victims, and in the corner and piled up like kindling, were three other bodies. What's more, they were conducting some bizarre kind of ritual. Something satanic or occult is what it says here in the file, with pentagrams or pentangles or whatever the fuck they are called, and lots of naked people. And running the show was a fifty one year old woman."

"You're kidding me?"

"I kid you not. And wait for this. She was a Dutch national who had moved to Finland after the war. Going by the name of Gerdi"

Pieter reached out for the file. "Give me that." He stared at the police mugshot, which showed a grey-faced lady with straggly white hair and bulging eyes looking straight back at the camera.

"And they caught them purely by chance?"

"Yes. They had no specific leads. Something led them to think it was going to be just another ordinary drugs bust, but what they found was something completely unexpected. A fantastic stroke of luck. It does happen sometimes."

"Like the cops who caught The Yorkshire Ripper."

"Exactly."

"So presumably there was a trial?"

"Yes, and it was quite a sensation at the time. All of the gory details came out and the press had a field day. Witnesses, the few they were, were threatened if they gave evidence, and some were later given new identities. Two of the jurors died in mysterious circumstances, they brought in experts on the occult and Wiccan magic, and there was talk of spells and curses. The Judge had some kind of mental breakdown: apparently he was found in his chambers one day babbling about strange smells and unearthly presences. Then, when they got onto the subject of motives, the main defendant, our friend Gerdi, she started on with some nonsense about opening portals to another dimension through the practice of ritualistic killings. Can you believe that rubbish? Throughout the course of the trial she was heard chanting incantations to herself."

Dyatlov paused then, and looked closely at Pieter.

"Are you ok?" he asked, concerned. "You look pale Van Dijk."

"I'm fine," he replied irritably.

Dyatlov and Floris exchanged a look.

"From the sound of it they didn't have much of a defence? That they were pretty much admitting to everything."

"Oh, they tried to defend what they'd done, from their own warped sense of perspective. But it wasn't the sort of legal defence that would stand up in court. Eventually their own lawyer just gave up and sat there squirming with embarrassment. It was obvious to everybody present that Gerdi was just batshit crazy."

"Crazy yes," put in Floris, "but very charismatic. She wasn't the first or the last to have that kind of hold over people. Or to be convinced that what they were doing, or hoping to achieve, was perfectly normal and rational to themselves. Nurse Beverley Allitt killed children because she suffered from Münchausen's Disease by Proxy, and thought she would be treated like a hero by bringing them back to life. Joachim Kroll was a German cannibal who killed over a dozen people in the 1950's and cut up their bodies to make a meat stew. Ed Gein turned his victims into lampshades and liked wearing human skin, and was the inspiration for Norman Bates and "Buffalo Bill"."

"Yes, thank you Adolf. The verdicts were a foregone conclusion. Guilty as hell. All of the bikers were imprisoned for life with no parole, while Gerdi was sent to a lunatic asylum."

"It says here that she killed herself a year later." Pieter was looking at a grainy photo in the file he held, which showed the figure of a woman hanging in her cell. "In 1982."

"And good riddance."

Pieter closed the file and tossed it onto his desk.

155

"But the case was never fully closed, despite what the Finnish police say. Some of the top detectives who worked on the case remained convinced that, even though she was an evil bitch, she wasn't the main mastermind behind the whole thing. That she was just a follower herself, like the biker gang, being used to do somebody else's bidding."

"The killings stopped with their convictions though?"

"Yes, in Finland at least. Perhaps the real culprits just went to ground. Look, I know it's only a tenuous link to our case, but with the Dutch connection and the motive, it's the best lead we have. And like Floris said earlier, he still has loads more papers to go through. He might find something else."

"I appreciate what you've done. You've come up with some good details Adolf. Keep digging for more."

Floris beamed up at him. He and Dyatlov started to clear up the boxes and loose papers lying around the office.

"That file has a condensed version of what we have found so far on this Finnish link. It's also duplicated on this laptop here. Go through it, it has lots more detail than what I've just outlined."

Pieter moved his chair from behind the door and let them out.

Alone again, Pieter reclaimed his desk and sat there going over their discussion.

Certainly the Finnish angle was worth pursuing. Perhaps he could speak to the senior investigator who handled the case back then, assuming he was still alive. Reading about old cases was always informative, but sometimes certain elements were lost or left out, especially the tiny nuances of a case, the feelings and thoughts of the people running the show. Personal theories would not always be recorded in the official files, particularly if they went against the accepted facts, and even more so once a case was closed with a successful conviction. Nothing beat talking to the actual people on the ground at the time.

He picked up the heavy file and flicked through it until he found the name of the senior investigator. There was no up-to-date contact details obviously, not for a case nearly forty years old, but there was a phone number for the Helsinki Police Foreign Liaison Office.

He was about to dial it when he noticed the time – 6:30pm

Best to wait until the morning.

Instead he went back to the segment of the file concerning the woman, Gerdi, the apparent leader of this group. Leader of their cult might be a better way of describing her. A cult with a bizarre and twisted outlook on life, obsessed with the occult.

There were a few more photos of her in addition to the police mugshot and picture of her body hanging in her cell. One showed her being taken into the courtroom, turning and grinning at the crowd of onlookers. Then there were a series of post mortem images, which he skipped through. Another one was taken on a family holiday when she was a young lady of about twenty, bending over to hold the hand of a toddler as they walked along a beach somewhere.

He guessed this must be her own child. Was she married? he wondered.

There was nothing in the file about her private life or marital status one way or the other, but there was something about her family. She'd had three children, one of which had passed away in the 1960's from polio, and two grandchildren. No details apart from one name.

A grandson, born in 1990.

Just a Christian name.

Bartholomew.

Pieter gently lowered the file and placed it onto the desk. In his chest something icy gave his heart the smallest of squeezes.

Slowly he came to his feet, the chair's legs scrapping backwards across the floor.

For about twenty seconds he stood motionless, not daring to blink or breathe.

HELSINKI – FINLAND. MAY 2002

The black Toyota with the tinted windows pulled up before the large security gate. The driver's window rolled down and a black-suited arm reached out towards the intercom system fixed to one of the stone pillars. A moment later, with a quiet electric hum, the gates slowly swung open, and the car glided forward down the short driveway towards the ornate house.

Swinging around the turning circle before a wide staircase, it drew to a halt, and the driver briskly jumped out to open the rear passenger door.

Three people stepped out. A smartly-dressed lady wearing an expensive looking coat and cream-coloured trousers, and two children, a boy and a girl.

The boy was the oldest, aged twelve, and full of confidence. He was quite tall for his age, if a little plump in the face. He stepped forward and then turned with an annoying sigh as he had to wait for the little girl who followed behind.

She was around six or seven years younger, and very pretty, with fine freckles across her nose, but was very shy by nature, and the lady had to usher her along and encourage her up the steps with the boy.

At the top the double doors of the large townhouse were already open and they stepped into the gloomy interior, leaving the spring sunshine behind.

The house was mostly silent. It was mid-morning, but instead of the hustle and bustle that one might expect, the place was still and hushed. There were no staff, or pets, to welcome the visitors, just a large empty hallway and its grand staircase leading up to a landing above.

The lady led them upwards. Their footsteps were cushioned by the thick, red carpet underfoot. Lining the walls were a number of paintings. One showed a grand seascape, another was of a lake surrounded by a majestic forest. Another was a portrait of a fine-looking fellow, resplendent in his military uniform. The boy and the girl gawped at them open-mouthed as they climbed past, but as they neared the top their attention switched to the landing just ahead.

At the top a long hallway stretched before them leading to an open doorway at the end, and even before they approached they heard the beeps and electronic buzzes of medical equipment, the hiss and gurgle of respirators.

Now the boy hung back as well as the little girl, but the lady escorting them gently encouraged them forward.

"I will be right here. In you go, both of you."

The room was carpeted in black, and the walls were of warm oak panelling. One whole side was dominated by a large, curved window, offering a panoramic view across the city.

At the centre was a king size bed surrounded by monitors and ventilators and syringe pumps, a resuscitator bag and a defibrillator and ICU screens.

On the bed, the dried-up old husk of a dying man.

The boy and the girl hesitated just inside the doorway. The room was large and spacious and beautifully adorned, with a high ceiling and fine furniture. In one corner was an ornate gilt mirror, and beyond it a private bathroom decorated with gold fittings and a grey slate floor. A bookcase was filled with old and rare volumes, preserved behind a glass front. But their attention was riveted on the man lying before them, and the sound of his slow and laboured breathing, which hissed through the oxygen mask hiding his features.

The old man opened his eyes. They scanned the room until they came to rest on the children and he beckoned them forward weakly.

The older boy and the young girl shuffled towards him reluctantly, until they stood on either side of the bed.

They watched him reach up and remove the oxygen mask, and the toothless grin beneath seemed more like a grimace of pain. A wracking cough crackled and wheezed from out of his emaciated body, and his other hand gripped the bedcovers tightly in discomfort, and the boy and girl waited nervously.

Eventually the convulsions passed and the skinny figure became still once more, but the eyes continued to look from face to face, and they seemed to shine with pride.

He exhaled slowly, and then spoke with surprising softness in a clear but whispery voice.

"My children, my lovely, sweet grandchildren."

The boy swallowed, for his throat had suddenly become dry, all of his earlier confidence gone. Confronted with the sight of this elderly man wasting away and dying before his eyes was a frightening experience. All the more so because they both knew who he was, had heard stories about him from their mother. And although they had never met him before, they had been filled with awe about today, a peculiar excitement that had built and built. They would finally get to see this powerful person, their grandfather, for themselves. The one who others spoke about in hushed and reverent tones.

Yet here he was, a weak and pitiful-looking shadow of a man, tired and decrepit and close to the end of his life.

The boy felt tears of shame and disappointment well up in his eyes. He felt let down, embarrassed and angry.

But the girl. Her heart bloomed with love and tenderness. An almost overwhelming and intoxicating feeling of compassion swelled inside her heart, and she stepped forward and smiled at her grandfather.

She lay her head gently on his chest. The rattling and wheezing coming from his worn-out lungs was frightening to her young mind, but she hugged him tightly anyway.

She felt him stroke her hair gently, his words soothing.

"Pass on what you learn. Pass on what you learn."

Then his hand squeezed her narrow shoulder tenderly, and she saw the ring on his finger, with its grinning skull leering back at her.

CHAPTER 17

BART AND THE NEWCASTLE BAR

Tuesday night at just after 7pm and things were thankfully quiet at The Newcastle Bar. Standing near the cars parked alongside the canal, Pieter could see through the large doors. Inside was just one customer, sitting at a table near the wall, nursing a beer and looking well on the way to being drunk.

That was good. The last thing he wanted was a packed out bar. Hopefully this could play out nice and calmly. If he was even right about this, which he sort of hoped he wasn't. After all, it wasn't that unusual a name in Holland, and there was a fifty/fifty chance that he'd got this completely wrong. But on the other hand, if he had read the situation correctly?

So best to go in softly, play the role of a man worried about his missing friend, and that he wasn't here to cause any more aggro. Simply ask a few questions, about Lotte and other loosely related matters, and see what kind of reaction he got.

Pieter moved towards the entrance, his hand subconsciously gliding across to the bulge of his firearm tucked underneath the bottom of his jacket in its holster, then unfastening the buttons at the front of his coat.

Steadying his breath, he stepped inside.

Bart was wiping down the bar and beer pumps with a wet cloth. As Pieter stepped nonchalantly forward, he looked up at him.

Scowling balefully, the barman folded up the cloth and placed it below the counter.

"You again?"

"Me again," Pieter answered.

There was a slight pause, and Pieter could feel his heart beating against his chest, noting too late that Bart's hands remained hidden out of sight behind the bar. They started to come up, holding something.

"So be it then, friend," Bart replied.

Bart pulled the trigger on the gun, and the bar erupted with the deafening explosive report.

The first round tore away Pieter's earlobe, splattering the back of his coat with blood and sinews of flesh. He barely had time to register the stinging burn before Bart fired twice more, round number two hitting the door to the toilets just behind Pieter, and the third shot punching a hole square through the forehead of the customer sipping his beer, killing him instantly.

Pieter staggered back, his head ringing and making him feel punch drunk. He watched as Bart spun away and dashed across the back of the bar, and then reach down to the floor to yank open the trapdoor leading to the beer cellar. He rushed down the steps, pausing for half a second to slap his palm against something on the wall on his way down, before disappearing through the opening.

Pieter quickly recovered from the shock. He took out his own firearm and dragged himself over the bar and tumbled in a heap on the far side. He scuttled forward towards the hole in the floor and peered cautiously over the edge.

A short flight of wooden steps led down. A bare bulb dangling from its flex lit the scene. At the bottom he could see the concrete base of the cellar and a couple of beer barrels, but not much else. On the wall at the side was a large red button. Fuck! An alarm of some sort. Bart had triggered an alarm.

"Put your gun down Bart!" he called out. "It's over! I don't want to have to kill you!"

There was no response.

Which meant he had no choice but to go down there after him.

With his gun pointing forward Pieter slowly eased himself down one slow step at a time, his whole body and mind tensed for more gunfire. Fully aware that in a confined space like a small beer cellar it would be almost impossible for Bart to miss him.

At the bottom he looked around. In addition to the beer barrels there were a couple of stacks of plastic crates leaning crazily against one wall. Other than that there was nothing. No sign of Bart, and nowhere for him to hide.

Then Pieter turned, and saw a small square opening in the bare wall behind the wooden steps. He crouched lower and passed below the wooden struts, and approached the black hole.

He peered inside, but it was too dark to see very far. Was Bart in there? He had to be.

Groping around in his trouser pocket, he pulled out his mobile and turned on the torch, and aimed the bright white light into the opening.

Stretching away into the distance was a narrow tunnel, with bare, damp walls. It twisted here and there, and sloped downwards into the ground, so that the end was lost from view.

Where did it lead?

How long had it been here?

Pieter considered turning back and calling for backup. That would be the rational thing to do. But as this was passing through his mind he heard a scurrying noise reach him from ahead, and then – and this chilled him to the bone – a crazy high pitched laughing, echoing and bouncing off the tunnel walls.

Pieter held back for a couple more seconds, and then he plunged into the tunnel after Bart.

The inside of the tunnel was tiny, perhaps four feet square, and he had to scurry along bent over in an awkward crouch with his head and back scraping across the roof. The walls were of stone as though it had been chiselled and cut straight through the bare rock.

The first few hundred feet sloped gently downwards. To begin with the floor and walls were just slightly damp, but the further, and deeper, he went the wetter the going became. After a couple of minutes he was splashing through puddles of mud, and icy drops of water were dripping down from above.

He had no idea where he was going. He tried to get a sense of direction, for, although there were a few twists and turns here and there, the route was essentially a straight one. Thinking back to the layout of the bar, the location of the cellar and the position of the tunnel opening, he thought he was headed generally southwards. Which meant he would be passing underneath the canal, hence the amount of water down here. But he was really only having a guess, and for all he knew he could be headed completely in the opposite direction.

Just then came that eerie laughter once more, the sound rolling and reverberating around the enclosed space, making it impossible to judge how far away, or close to him, Bart was.

After a few more minutes the tunnel levelled off and he paused to get his breath. He still had a hold of his gun in one hand and the mobile with its torch in the other. The beam of white light only penetrated two or three metres ahead, and beyond that there was pitch darkness, hiding anyone who might be lurking there.

Again he wondered if he should summon some help, but when he glanced down at his mobile phone he saw he had no bars, therefore zero reception, so it was too late for that now, and too late to go back. So on he went, the torch light jumping and bouncing around off the tunnel walls, creating a jerky world of light and dark.

His ear hurt like hell and he was starting to get winded and wondering just how far the tunnel went, when finally the floor cantered upwards. It gave him renewed vigour, so he pushed on up the gentle incline.

The tunnel became even narrower. The walls and floor and roof closed in, and he had to crawl on his hands and knees now. To make his progress easier he slipped his gun back into its holster.

It became even steeper, and tighter still, until he was on his belly and pulling and dragging himself along with his hands, with the toes of his shoes seeking a purchase and pushing hard. He wondered how the hell Bart had got through with his huge bulk and height.

Finally after an age he noticed the roof of the tunnel disappear, and the end of the tunnel came up on him nearly by surprise, and he tumbled over the rim of the exit onto the floor two feet below. Carefully he stood up and looked at his surroundings.

Turning a full circle the torch revealed a square, brick chamber. In one wall was an old iron door, with large studs dotted over its surface. It was set just above the level of the floor and seemed to have flanges around its edges, a little like a ship's hatchway. There was a small circular handle, which he guessed was spun left or right to lock and unlock the door. At the moment it was open slightly, but Pieter could see nothing through the narrow gap.

Near the centre of the room were a number of wooden chairs, arranged in a circle and facing each other. In the centre of the circle was a round pit, around six feet in diameter. Pieter approached it to see how deep it was or what lay down there, and when he pointed the beam of the torch on it he wished he hadn't. At the bottom, cemented into the base with short chains, were four iron manacles. They looked to have red rust marks on them, or at least that's what Pieter told himself they were. The pit itself was no more than three feet deep, and in one of its curved walls was a small grate.

He shook his head, trying not to dwell too much on the pit's purpose, and he moved away, noticing as he did that beside one of the chairs was a long handle standing upright out of the stone floor, similar to a railroad switch.

Just then he heard faint voices, and he turned towards the door. They seemed to be coming from there.

Again he trod carefully as he walked across, afraid of making any sound. As he neared the door the voices rose in volume, then quietened, rose and fell, and it became clear what he was hearing.

From the other side of the door, drifting through the narrow gap, he could hear chanting.

A faint glow showed through the opening, casting enough light for him to see without needing the torch on his mobile. He put it away and drew out his gun again, and, gripping the iron flange around the door, he drew it open.

On the other side were three steps leading up to a short passageway. It was lined with a red carpet, and on either side was a double row of wall sconces holding lit torches. A heavy drape covered the far end of the passageway.

Pieter climbed the short flight of stairs and started forward. The chanting was growing louder now, more insistent, as though building up to something.

He paused just this side of the drapes, wondering whether to burst in and use the element of surprise or perhaps he should wait and see what happened, maybe try and sneak a peek into the room beyond. However, he didn't have time to ponder his choices for long, for just then a strong arm reached around from behind and gripped him suddenly in a powerful neck lock, squeezing hard, and at the same time the muzzle of a gun pushed against his neck just behind his throbbing ear.

"Drop your weapon, you cunt," a harsh voice whispered, Bart's hot breath against his skin.

Pieter had no idea where he'd come from, there must have been a hidden alcove that he'd walked straight by or something. He thought about resisting, kicking out, but then two more figures hove into view, one to either side. These were holding wicked-looking hand-scythes which glinted in the torch-light, and covering their faces were carved wooden masks with a pair of straight brown horns sticking up from their heads, and straggly hair like an animals mane. Through their eye slits and mouths Pieter could see the faces behind the masks, staring blankly at him.

"Do it, or they'll slit you open."

Pieter threw his gun aside, and sagged against the big man behind him, and the pressure against his neck eased, but only a little.

Bart forced him forward, keeping the gun against his neck, and they passed through the curtain just as the chanting came to a sudden stop, the silence filling the room beyond.

He found himself in a large, circular space. The floor was covered in more red carpet, and the plaster walls were painted cream, and affixed with more burning torches. Above, high up near the ceiling and spaced evenly around the circumference, were a number of narrow window slits, dark now that night had fallen. Over to the left and right were two large arched openings, like two semi-circle eye-slits, with shadowy chambers beyond. Inside, amid the gloom, Pieter could make out several shelves and wooden boxes, and the walls right at the back were lined with hundreds of tiny holes. Within each one, hundreds of human skulls looked back at him through their empty eye-sockets.

Some kind of catacomb, they were in some kind of old, cobwebby catacomb filled with the bones of the dead.

A circle of people stood waiting for him. They were all dressed in long, dark robes covered in gold symbols and markings and crescent moon shapes and stars, tied at the waist with rope. There were about a dozen of them, and each wore carved demon masks identical to the other two. All except one. Standing directly opposite Pieter across the far side of the circle of people was a robed figure wearing a goat's skull in place of their own head, the long pointy snout and narrow nostrils and large black eye sockets appraising him silently. Huge horns grew out from the temples, to curve down to the sides. On the bony forehead, in blood, an inverted pentagram.

Pieter felt his legs go weak, and he might have gone down had Bart not had such a firm hold of him.

Again he urged Pieter forward, a tiny snicker coming from his lips, and the circle on this side parted to allow them through, before closing behind them again.

Seated in the centre, arms and legs tied to a chair, head covered in a hessian sack, was the naked figure of a man.

The goat-headed person lifted their arms and opened them wide in greeting, and the voice, although muffled by the skull, was instantly recognizable.

"Welcome," Lotte said. "You are just in time."

CHAPTER 18

A HISTORY OF FAMILY MADNESS

Lotte made the sign of the cross, inverted, and everybody followed suit.

"Bring him forward," she ordered, her voice now strong and powerful, and Bart manhandled Pieter towards the centre of the circle of hooded people, and then forced him to his knees.

He watched mesmerized and numb and confused and terrified in equal measure as she stepped forward and placed her hands on the shoulders of the man seated on the chair. Her touch made him jump, and Pieter could hear his breath coming in quick gasps now, the sacking over his head moving as he twisted his head from side to side.

"I see you have managed to find us, thanks to Bart leading you here? My loyal servant, my loyal brother."

Pieter snapped his head around to catch a quick glimpse of the barman, who was smiling broadly, his eyes watery with love and devotion.

"Your brother? But you told me… you told me he hurt you? That he…" His voice trailed off in despair.

Lotte was shaking her head. "Oh you fool. Our ruse was so simple, and you fell for it. I'm sorry for the deceit and lies, but they were necessary to entice you and to draw you into our game. Bart would never hurt me. He loves me."

Bart moved away from Pieter and joined his sister. She slipped an arm around his big waist and kissed him on the lips with her goat-snout

169

face, making Pieter sick to the stomach. The two henchmen with the scythes took up position just behind Pieter.

Lotte turned her skull-face back towards him, and now her voice had an edge to it. "But you weren't supposed to hurt him so badly. You were only meant to warn him, not beat him. You monster!" The irony of her words was breathtaking.

"You fucking mad bitch," Pieter mumbled to himself, shaking his head. "You're fucking mad."

"I can understand how it might look, from your point of view. And I was reluctant to use you like that. I do genuinely like you Pieter, and I was hoping you would become a willing participant in our wonderful project. Alas, despite my best attempts to entice you and seduce you, you proved difficult to manipulate. So we had to use other methods. Therefore, we set out to play you – I hate that expression, but it seems appropriate here – we set out to draw you in by approaching things in a more oblique way, using emotional distress to weaken your defences."

"I have no idea what you are talking about." He tried to rise, but a pair of strong hands pushed down on his shoulders, keeping him there.

"Your father, oh, that was a necessary evil, but it worked. Your distress and grief was palpable, and it was the opening I required."

Pieter wasn't sure he was hearing right. His father? What did his death have to do with… the thought evaporated like mist as a horrible realization started to dawn on him.

"Yes, a tragedy, mmm, but nobody will miss a drunken old man like that, apart from yourself of course. He was a waste of humanity, a drain on the world, and on you. In time you'll come to thank us for what we did."

Pieter wanted to throw up. He also wanted to grip her by the neck and squeeze the life out of her.

"It was an accident, he drowned," Pieter whispered hoarsely.

"Perhaps you need to hear the truth." Lotte pointed across to one of the robed figures – one of her followers, Pieter now realized – and beckoned them forward. "Tell him."

He turned his head and watched as one of those making up the circle stepped forward and removed their carved demon mask. His heart sank as he looked across at the familiar face.

Famke, now bright-eyed, her features fully alert and showing none of the haggard and washed out signs of someone dependent on alcohol, now with her hair clean and shining. Pretty and elegant Famke. Not Famke the drunk.

Christ, how could they have fooled him so easily, so totally?

He had known her for years, had seen her sink to the same level of human misery as his dad. Watched her drink herself into oblivion, smelt the booze on her breath, on her clothes, seen her lying in her own vomit. But all a ruse. All an act, tricking his dad and using him and destroying him, all just a deception to set Pieter up.

"Go on Famke," urged Lotte, "explain to Pieter here how easy it was."

Famke turned her gaze onto Pieter and now her eyes blazed with madness, a crazy zeal that seemed to leap from her body in waves, and her lip curled up in an ugly snarl.

"That idiot, that smelly old man, that pitiful, weeping, pathetic cretin! He gave me the perfect opportunity to do what I needed to do. 'Let's go fishing' he said. 'We can take the boat out, catch something for supper. It will be romantic'. Ha! I even tried to stop him, to talk him out of it, I don't know why, but I did. But you know what your father was like, once he got an idea in his head there was no changing his mind. So I gave in, let him have it his way, on the condition that he be careful and not fall in."

Bart, standing beside his sister, tittered quietly.

"So out we went, right into the middle of the river, two old drunks in charge of a leaky old boat at midnight. All I had to do was keep the drinks flowing, and your father, oh how he kept on drinking and drinking into the night. I was literally pouring it down his scrawny neck. And we sang, it was an hilarious sight, there we were staggering about on the deck, singing our hearts out and dancing away like two rock-a-billy old farts. Your father showing off as usual, jigging about near the side, and, oh dear, there was silly old me stumbling and tripping into him, and there he was flapping his arms about in a panic, but still laughing his head off, so I gave him another little push and dearie me, over the side he went."

There was a total stillness in the room now, everybody hypnotized by Famke's words, and Pieter squeezed his eyes tight, his lips trembling with emotion.

"There was such a splash, I felt sure somebody on shore would have heard, especially when he popped up like a floaty old turd and started screaming his little head off. He was crying, shouting for me to help, so I joined in, bawling away just like him, 'help me Famke!' I copied him, 'help me, I'm drowning!!' You should have seen the look on his face when he heard me. But the best part, Oh you'll laugh when you hear this, the best bit was when he managed to splash his way back to the boat and grabbed a hold of the side, scrabbling away to get a good grip, so what did sweet little Famke do? It was just too tempting, I couldn't help myself I'm afraid, with those little wiggly piggly fingers right in front of my feet, and I – oh, this was so naughty of me – I trod on them, and they went pop under my shoes, and he yelped like a pup and so I scrunched on his fingers even harder, until he slipped back and under the surface, floating down into the dark with his mouth open and filling with dirty, smelly water."

Famke paused for dramatic effect, looking directly at Pieter who had opened his eyes again.

"I watched him go down," she whispered, with a ridiculous tear in her eye, "his white splotchy face looking right back at me, until he was gone."

She sighed heavily, then shrugged her shoulders.

Bart gave a girly little snicker again.

Then quietness that was so taut Pieter could feel the vibrating of the very air.

"Why?" he asked in a hushed voice. He gazed at Famke, and turned back to Lotte, searching for her eyes through the goat-skull's sockets. "Why? What are you hoping to achieve? You're all stark raving mad, but why are you doing all of this?"

"Power." Lotte's voice rang hollow around the room. "To gain the ultimate knowledge. To seek a path to a lower plane of existence. Death to bring a new form of life."

She moved about, walking back and forth, but with her gaze always on him.

"We don't pursue sacrifice for joy or fun. We gain no pleasure in the shedding of blood. A means to an end, that is why we do the terrible things we do. It's been tried before. Aleister Crowley, the Grand Master of The Golden Dawn, he tried in Paris in 1914, but he failed. Then it was tried again during the war and also in Finland during the 1970's, but again this met with failure. But we," she swept her arm across the circle of people, "we have finally achieved what others were unable to. We have opened the way to enlightenment. We have raised life from death."

She stepped around the man seated in the chair, who was quivering with terror, and approached Pieter until she was face to face with him, her eyes looking through her mask and seeking his.

"We have raised the dead Pieter. From this very place. We have accomplished the impossible."

Through gritted teeth Pieter hissed back, "I'll fucking kill you. You crazy, deranged psycho!" He spat at the goat-skull.

Lotte ignored him and turned away. "This place. Do you know what it was once used for? No, you probably don't even know where you are. Well, let me enlighten you. The building above us, above the catacombs here, it was originally one of the old city gates and part of the defensive wall surrounding Amsterdam during the fifteenth century. The Sea Dike which kept the flood waters back went right by this location. Merchants would come and go, and pay their taxes and weigh their goods here, to keep Amsterdam thriving as one of the world's biggest sea ports. Later, it was used by the Surgeon Guild as an anatomic theatre where they performed public dissections. Lecturers and medical students would come to watch corpses being cut open, and afterwards the bodies would be stored down here in the crypt. Hundreds of them, lining the walls in this secret catacomb. There they are Pieter, look at them. But thanks to our achievements they no longer remain at rest. Can you imagine that? Life from Death? To gain the ultimate knowledge we desire we must raise life from death!"

She tilted her head, smiling through the jaw bone.

"Your father doesn't need to stay dead forever."

Pieter moved as if to lunge forward and jump on her, but a pair of strong arms hauled him back and one of the men at his side brought up his wicked-looking scythe and pointed the sharp tip at Pieter's throat.

"Hold him there," Lotte ordered them. "He will witness for himself how we can realize this marvellous feat."

She clicked her fingers and someone stepped forward. From within the folds of their dark robe they produced a small hypodermic needle. Pieter thought at first that it was meant for him, some kind of drug to either subdue him or knock him out, but instead the masked figure bent forward near the naked man sitting in the chair and injected something directly into his penis. Pieter cringed, wondering what the hell was happening, and the man panicked, his breath coming through the sack in quick and short bursts.

After a moment he settled. Still conscious, but calm.

Lotte in the meantime had drifted across to stand before her brother. She turned and unfastened the rope around her waist, and then shrugged out of her robe to reveal her full nakedness to the gathering. Bart, a big leering grin on his face, feasted his gaze over her naked flesh and reached out to cup one of her breasts in his huge hand. She gently slapped his hand away. "Not now," she told him mildly. "Later."

Watching this, Pieter felt revulsion flip his stomach over, leaving him queasy. He averted his gaze, but now saw that the man seated at the centre of the circle of people was now fully aroused. Whatever they had injected him with it had sexually stimulated him thus, in spite of the terror he must be feeling.

With a sense of the inevitable he now found it impossible not to watch, no matter how repulsive he found the whole episode. It was like being witness to a terrible road accident or an act of frightful violence: even though your natural compassion told you it was wrong to look, you did so anyway.

Lotte looked over, her eyes flashing through her mask. "This should have been you having the honour of sharing your life force Pieter. Instead I had to visit you in your dreams."

She moved across to the man tied to the chair, and turned to face away from him, so those gathered could bear full witness. Parting her legs, she lowered herself onto him, a quiet sigh escaping her lips. The man grunted in response.

Lotte glided up and down, her rhythm slow and smooth as her moistness eased the sexual act, but after a few moments her pace increased and her breathing became louder, together with her gentle moans. Throughout, she maintained eye contact with Pieter. Then she was squirming on the man's erectness and her tempo became fast and frantic, and the man was thrusting into her.

"Come on," Lotte was grunting, "come on," and she was breathing hard through her nostrils, becoming more like the animal she was portraying, the goat-skull tilting back as she peaked, and the man cried out in simultaneous ecstasy.

Lotte remained there, her chest rising and falling as she gradually recovered from her exertion, the man still inside her. Then, when she was finished, she pushed herself to her feet. Walking back over to Bart, she ran her hand across his stomach, and once again his beady eyes were transfixed by her body. Then he leaned down to listen as she whispered instructions to him through the muzzle of the skull.

Bart dutifully moved across to the seated man and, grabbing the top of the hessian sacking, he pulled it free and tossed the material aside.

Underneath, the bald-headed man was weeping and trembling and he could not bring himself to glance up, so complete was his shame.

"I'm sorry Inspector," officer Joos murmured, his drugged voice sounding all slurred. "They jumped me on my way home from work. They came out of nowhere."

Pieter felt such sorrow in his helplessness he could think of nothing to say.

"Bart, shut him up!"

Her brother made a small signal with his hand and the two henchmen holding the scythes moved towards Joos, their weapons held high, bringing a cry of terror from the policeman's lips.

"No!" shouted Pieter. "Don't! Leave him alone, it's me you want!"

Bart, who was enjoying the whole spectacle, shouted back, "It's not you she wants, it's what you have in your balls that's important!"

"Lotte, please!"

It was no good. The two masked figures – he assumed they were men from their gait and build – unleashed their pent up excitement and launched themselves at Joos, attacking him in a crazy blood-lust of violence, hacking and slashing. Joos screamed in agony, and he thrashed his body in a futile attempt to escape his bonds, and as they cut and chopped his cries of pain became pleads as he begged them to stop, and the sound of his death-cries echoed and bounced off the walls and ceiling. He whimpered as fountains of red sprayed and drenched the two robed men, and then he was twitching and fell quiet, until the only noise was the sickening ripping of flesh as the butchery went on. Finally they stopped, but only from sheer exhaustion, and they stood looking at their handiwork and panting for breath.

Lotte again made the sign of an inverted cross and moved away into the shadows of one of the alcoves.

Pieter stared down at the floor in abject defeat.

The circle of robed figures started to quietly chant, their incantation almost sounding like a hum of electric energy, and they slowly swayed from side to side. The temperature in the room seemed to suddenly drop, until the air was chilled. Pieter could feel goose bumps on his arms, and the hairs at the base of his scalp became brittle like minute icicles.

There was a rattle of something moving, a dragging of feet and a crunching like someone walking over autumn twigs, and Pieter lifted his head and turned towards the sound, seeing Lotte reappear from the shadows. She was holding something to her body, something brown and thin, held together with shredded and tattered cloth. Pieter saw the legs and the rib bones, the thin and rotten arms that she held out, the human skull lolling back against her breasts with its jaw grinning as though in pleasure.

She stepped into the circle of chanting followers holding the human skeleton to her body, and she swayed in ecstasy, crying in pleasure through the goat-skull she still wore, moving the dead and lifeless body in a mad parody of life, dancing a macabre dance of death.

CHAPTER 19

FLORIS de KOK (ADOLF)

It was 9pm and Floris de Kok was still working down in his private office on the basement level. On the floor beside his small desk he had stacked the large box files containing the paperwork from the Finland case. On the room's only spare chair, which he'd wheeled across, was a thick pile of cardboard slipcases, which he wanted close to hand as he worked his way through the details of the murders and subsequent trial perpetrated by the occultist, Gerdi, and her cult members during the 1970's and 80's.

At the moment he was reading through the list of known assets and properties and business interests connected to her and her family members.

In truth there wasn't much.

The Finnish police had very little information about Gerdi at all. They did not have her exact date of birth – although it was guessed at being sometime around about 1930 – nor did they have any real knowledge about where she was born. They knew she was from Holland, and there was mention of a convent somewhere near the border with Germany, but whether she had been born there or ended up being raised as an orphan there was not clear.

At the time of her arrest it was clear that she was a woman of means. She held 25% shares in two large companies: Metsä Electro Energies and O P Group Medical, as well as business interests in heavy construction projects. Her husband – name unknown – was chairman of FCone Software, an early computer industries working group. Upon her conviction and subsequent death her shares had passed to her children, principally her daughter. The trail went quiet after this, but the next known facts stated that around about 2002, the family estate, a large house on the outskirts of Helsinki, was signed over to her grandchildren, even though they were both minors: a boy aged twelve and a girl aged five.

However, they did not stay here for long. As soon as the boy turned eighteen the property was sold, and he and his sister, together with their mother, moved to Amsterdam.

Things became hazy at this point once again.

It was thought that with their substantial wealth, the family purchased more property throughout the city. Two particular properties caught Floris's attention:

A business premises in the Red Light District which five years ago was granted a licence to sell alcohol. The bar was leased under the name of a male individual – Bartholomew Janssen.

And here, in this file, was another property owned by the same individual: Schreierstoren, better known as Weeping Tower. The location of yesterday's shootout!

Floris sat up straight in his chair. The lease ran out last year and the building had since remained empty, but surely this was too much of a coincidence?

There was nothing else about this Bartholomew Janssen so he went back to the file index to see if there was anything in there about his younger sister who, from his quick mental calculation, would be in her early twenties by now. Yet he found nothing, he didn't even have a first name for her.

Instead, feeling a frisson of excitement start to pass through him, which in turn set his arm off trembling, Floris booted up his computer and immediately found the police database containing public records on building ownership/leases and the District Probate Registry. Technically, as a civilian employee, he shouldn't be doing this, but what the hell?

When the system was up he typcd in **BARTHOLOMEW JANSSEN**. The same two entries came up: The Newcastle Bar and Schreierstoren Tower. But there was a link to another individual.

CHARLOTTE JANSSEN.

With it, two property leases.

One for a flat in De Gooyer, which was listed as her place of residency.

And another for…

He leaned close to the computer monitor, wondering if he'd read it right.

"Bingo."

Adolf ran for the stairs.

CHAPTER 20

THE WAAG

You see? You see? Life from death!" sang Lotte, as she danced around the room with the lifeless corpse.

Pieter could virtually smell the sweat of insanity oozing out of her pores, but he was transfixed by the sickening spectacle. The robed figures continued to chant and sway and some of them lifted their masked faces to the ceiling as though in the throes of ecstasy. Their arms came up, beseeching the heavens. It was bizarre and frantic and horribly deranged, unlike anything in his past experience.

He could feel how intoxicating the atmosphere was, perhaps it was a form of mass hysteria, but one look at the mutilated body of Officer Joos belayed any notion of other-worldly powers. This was murder pure and simple, fed by psychotic madness yes, but executed with merciless violence.

He watched as Lotte swirled in front of him. She was laughing now, the sound of her voice deep and hollow in the skull. Gradually she slowed down, gliding smoothly across the room and then went past him, and Pieter turned to watch as she disappeared through the curtained doorway behind him, still embracing the skeletal remnants.

Strong hands grabbed him from behind then, and he looked to see Bart had a hold of him. He wrapped his huge arms around Pieter and clasped his hands together across Pieter's chest, locking his arms to his sides in a vice-like grip. Trapped like this, Pieter could do nothing as Bart used his huge bulk and strength to bodily lift him from his feet, and carried him through the curtains after Lotte. Behind them, the masked followers came in a line, suddenly quiet.

Along the short and carpeted passageway, then down the small flight of steps, and through the large iron doorway back into the small square room. The others filed in behind them, some holding flickering torches that they'd removed from the walls outside, and in their orange glow Pieter saw again the circle of chairs surrounding the pit in the floor.

Lotte was seated in one of the chairs. She had removed the goat-skull, and she smiled beatifically at him. In the chair beside her was the decomposing corpse, the bones and old garments slumped down in the seat. In the flickering torchlight its empty eye sockets seemed to move, as though watching Pieter.

Someone handed back her robe and she slipped it around her shoulders. Several of the masked figures seated themselves, and the rest, those holding the torches, took up positions around the walls.

Bart carried Pieter towards the edge of the circular pit. Glancing down, Pieter once again saw the manacles there, and his stomach knotted with mounting fear.

Bart flung him down into the hole and then jumped in after him. Pieter tried to rise, but the other man's strength was too immense, and although he struggled and tried to resist, it was all too easy for Bart to force him down. First he manacled his left ankle, and then his right, and then he did the same to his wrists, the last iron clasp snapping shut with a resounding snap. Bart then jumped back out and dusted off his hands with a satisfied look on his smug face.

Pieter lay there on his back with his arms and legs spread-eagled. From his position, and because of the lip of the round pit, he could not see the legs of those seated, just their upper bodies.

Silence had fallen. Nobody spoke or sang, and everybody was still. The only sound Pieter could hear was the thudding of his heart, beating faster and faster in his ears. His eyes darted from face to face, seeing all of the demon masks looking down at him. Even the corpse seemed to have tilted its head for a look. Pieter's gaze came back to Lotte.

She wasn't smiling anymore. Her small mouth was a narrow slit in the centre of her beautiful face. She looked sad, her eyes pitying. There was a tiny crease between her brows.

When she spoke, breaking the quiet, her voice was a mere whisper.

"Life from death and death from life."

She reached out a hand and grasped the handle beside her chair, and with a grinding of metal, she yanked it back in one solid movement.

There was a small sound beside his ear. Pieter turned his head, and saw the tiny grate that he'd noticed earlier, just in the side of the pit, he saw it turn and open. There was a gurgling, then water started to pour out through the grate. He felt it swirl around his body, the coldness making him catch his breath, and it swished as more and more poured out of the hole. As it started to slowly fill the bottom of the pit, getting deeper and deeper, Pieter suddenly understood and a blind panic seized him.

He pulled his body hard against his restraints, lifting his body upwards, but the chains securing the manacles into the concrete base of the pit were very short, mere inches in length, and he could barely move. Not even enough to raise himself into a sitting position. He looked around desperately, thinking fast. Where the hell was the water coming from? The grate must open into a small pipe, which fed water probably from the canal. Lotte pulling the handle had obviously opened a valve. Was there a drainage hole of some sort? Surely there had to be?

Pieter glanced down between his feet and saw a small, square-shaped metal plate set flat into the concrete base. On the top was a rusty-looking ring, no doubt used to pull the plate up and empty out the water. But there was no way he could do that, not chained and restrained like this. This led him to one incontestable conclusion.

He was in serious trouble.

Lifting his head he looked towards Lotte again.

"Listen, don't do this. This is fucking crazy."

Her eyes considered him, but now they were as blank as her face.

"You'll never get away with this. Cop killers never do. You'll go down for life, you'll never see the light of day again."

Still he received no response, so now he looked around at the circle of seated people, at their inscrutable, demon-masked faces. "None of you will! If the police don't just kill you first! Listen to me, what she's doing is crazy, all of this crap isn't going to bring that thing back to life! She's just using you, she thinks you're stupid fools, to be used in her crazy scheme! And when she's done with you, she'll just throw you aside! You mean nothing to her, you're like shit on her shoe!! God damn it, don't just fucking sit there and let this happen!"

Nothing. Not so much as a flicker of movement. They were as still as the corpse sitting alongside them.

And by now the water was splashing over his legs and arms, and up across his chest and around his hair and jaw.

Pieter yanked at his chains, he twisted and pulled and strained with every bit of strength, and he lifted his head clear of the rising water and craned his neck to lift his shoulders up off the concrete base. The chains didn't budge at all. He arched his back and kicked back and forth with his legs. He sagged again, noticing the water was close to reaching the level of his face, so he pulled once more, but to no avail.

He sank back down. His breathing was coming fast now as fear seized him, water was gurgling over his cheeks and across his mouth and nostrils, so he spat it out, and lifted his head up as far as he could.

Jesus!

Above him, the circle of onlookers watched in silence.

*   *   *

In keeping with his style of leadership Dyatlov led the assault from the front.

The three separate teams – Red, Black and Zero 1 – had gathered on the cobbles of Nieuwmarkt, where during the daytime the wooden market stalls stood. At this time of night they had been packed away, and any members of the public strolling across the large open space had quietly but forcefully been asked to leave, and the surrounding streets closed off. Then, with his squad leaders gathered around, the former Russian Spetnaz officer had issued final instructions.

Red Team, which he would lead, were designated the primary assault squad, and were made up of fifteen men. They would enter their target through the large red doors at the front of the building, beneath the big overhanging canopy. They would secure the ground floor and the lower level. Black Team would gain entry through two smaller doors around the back, and their task was to clear the upper floors. Zero 1, consisting of twenty men, were to be held in reserve, and their job was to remain outside and to be ready to offer assistance when and where it might be needed. This team would also cover all possible escape routes out of the large building should any of the bad guys manage to get away. Zero 1 had a number of medics in their squad too, and once Phase 1 of the assault was over these individuals would move in to tend to the wounded. Police casualties were anticipated to be high.

Their target was the huge building that dominated the market square. It had the appearance of a small castle. At the centre was one huge circular turret capped by a massive slate roof pointing into the sky. Positioned at equidistant points around its circumference were four smaller and narrower turrets, with a large square blocky keep jutting out between two of these, which contained the front entrance. Red-shuttered windows covered the whole edifice.

At various times during its life, the building had served as a medieval city gate, where merchants would have their goods weighed. It had also been used as a place where surgeons and medical students performed public dissections. For a while it was the site where murderers and thieves would be executed, their heads lobbed off with a guillotine on the cobbled square. More latterly it was renovated as a popular café where tourists and office workers would gather for lunch. Named The Waag, it was one of Amsterdam's principal sightseeing spots. Crazy to think that it was currently being used as the main HQ for the most wanted criminals in The Netherlands, who were hiding right in the heart of the city.

With their instructions received and passed on to their men, the two main assault squads quietly took up position. Wearing breathing masks and night-vision goggles, the heavily armed men placed small directional explosive charges on their designated entry-points, and set the timers at ten seconds.

In near-perfect synchronization the charges blew in a huge rippling, explosive blast that crashed out over the square. The shock wave blew out several windows of nearby buildings and set off multiple car alarms. The doors of the building caved inwards, blown off their hinges, and Dyatlov, being the first man, threw in first a flash-bang and then a tear gas/smoke grenade, and went charging through the entrance with his assault rifle tucked into his shoulder. Without needing to look he knew his men were right behind him.

The series of powerful explosions shook the huge building, causing the ancient walls to shudder, and trickles of dust fell from the ceiling of the small room onto those seated below. A grinding and rending noise came from the passage just outside, and more dust billowed through the iron doorway in a dense cloud.

For a handful of seconds nobody moved, frozen rigid with shock.

Then Lotte came to her feet, and her countenance had changed: now a heavy scowl marred her beautiful features, a furious anger bubbling to the surface.

"They're here," she spat. "Bart! Arm our people!"

Bart, who was the only one grinning with the thrill of what was happening, pointed down into the pit, at the chained-up man now completely submerged under the water. "What about him?"

"Forget him. He'll be dead in a minute anyway. Go! Go! Your sister is in danger!"

This was enough to spur Bart into action. He took one final glance down at the thrashing, drowning figure, and then charged through the iron door. The robed men and women followed him, along the short passage where part of the ceiling had come down and back through the curtain into the larger round room. He led them underneath one of the arches leading to the catacombs. Here was a small wooden door set into the old stone wall, and he pulled this open and darted into the storage room beyond. This was their arsenal, rack after rack of modern assault rifles, semi-automatics, Uzi snub-nosed machine guns, grenades, RPG's and SA-7 Grail shoulder-launched missiles, Russian-made RPK light machine guns, plastic explosives, handguns of numerous kind, and tens of thousands of rounds of ammunition. Bart went to the nearest gun rack and started handing them out. Other robed figures went over to the locked cases and filled their pockets with grenades and magazines of ammunition, whatever they could grab their hands on. The building was large, a veritable rabbit-warren of corridors and annexes and staircases and hidden alcoves, and they each knew the place like the back of their hands. Anybody assaulting the place would find themselves heading into a death trap. They may have breached the entrances, but after that, they would pay for every inch of ground they gained in blood.

Pieter was aware that something was going on. He'd felt the concrete beneath him shudder, and the water in the pit had washed violently from side to side, some of it splashing out onto the floor of the room. This was a godsend – if only a brief one – for suddenly his face was clear of the water as the level dropped several inches. He snatched in great gulps of air, coughing and gasping, and when the water cleared from his eyes he saw that the room was now empty of people. He looked around, but from down in the pit he couldn't really see much, apart from the rotting corpse still sitting there. The others, including Lotte, had fled.

Yet lying there and still chained to the floor, with the water still gushing out through the grate, his respite was set to be short-lived.

Once the reverberations from the blasts echoed away, the silence inside seemed just as deafening to Dyatlov. He moved forward cautiously. The smoke was so thick that without the night-vision goggles clamped over his eyes, he doubted he be able to see anything. As it was, the world was a strange, flickering green-coloured place, criss-crossed with the beams from his and his men's laser sights.

Sliding down one wall, and with another assault-team member similarly hugging the opposite wall, he eased forward along a short corridor.

Part way down, the passage was interrupted with a short flight of stairs going upwards, before the corridor continued, then disappeared around a bend to the right.

There was no sound of fighting coming from anywhere else in the building, no shooting or yelling or more flash-bangs going off. Just this peculiar quietness.

Dyatlov froze. Footsteps somewhere, rushing up a staircase from the sound of it. Then running feet overhead. He jerked a thumb upwards, indicating the floor above them. Black Team should be up there dealing with that. Their job was here on the ground-floor level, as well as down in the basement area.

He finally reached the turn in the corridor and he whipped around the wall, aiming straight ahead. A closed door confronted him at the end, and he and his squad approached cautiously.

In the wall behind them a hidden panel slid silently aside.

Three or four masked figures wearing their dark robes emerged from the shadows, raised their guns, and opened fire into the backs of the knot of police just ahead.

The corridor erupted with violence and noise. Taken completely by surprise, a handful of Dyatlov's men went down in a spray of blood. The sound of gunfire and screaming overwhelmed his senses, and this was taken up throughout the building as the din of battle shattered the tension.

Dyatlov, being at the front, was shielded by those behind, and he spun and ducked. There was total pandemonium in the corridor, with several of his men lying prostrate on the floor. Charging towards them were three figures dressed in bizarre robes, their faces hidden behind dark masks. As they ran full pelt along the hall they were firing from the hip, the muzzle-flashes blinding him through his goggles.

Dyatlov fired on instinct, preying he didn't hit any of his own men, and was rewarded with the sight of two of their attackers going down. A third was flung back against the wall, two red bullet holes blooming across their chest. Slowly their legs buckled and they slid down to the floor, leaving a slick trail of blood on the wall.

The corridor was thick with swirling smoke but the shooting here had stopped. Elsewhere he could hear the sound of prolonged firing, plus the dull concussion of grenades. Over his communications ear-piece came shouted instructions and warnings, relayed from the fighting above:

"Shooters to the left!"

"Room clear! Two down, condition unknown!"

"Grenade, grenade!" Another thud of an explosion. "Six in the corridor, three on the stairs. Zero 1, send a half squad!"

Fuck! Dyatlov thought. What a fucking shit storm!

He made a snap decision. He ordered four of his squad to proceed through the closed door they had been approaching, while he and the two remaining men would come with him through the secret panel from where the gunmen had appeared. Wherever it led to. As for their wounded, protocol was for them to press on regardless, and not to stop and administer medical aid.

Dyatlov stepped around the dead and dying and tried to ignore the moans of agony. As he passed by he again noted the robed figure slumped down in a sitting position against the wall. The person's demon-mask had fallen away, and he saw the face underneath was that of a young woman, perhaps only a teenager, with short hair and a deathly-white face.

Dyatlov shrugged inwardly. This was no time for introspection. They had a job to do.

Carefully he and his two team-members stepped through the wood panel.

On the other side, a set of stone steps led downwards. Part way down was a small landing, and a turn, before they continued to the basement level.

Leading the way, Dyatlov slowly descended, his breath coming in harsh gasps and his heart pounding in his chest. He reached the landing and was about to continue when a sudden burst of automatic fire opened up on them from below, shattering the wall just inches from his head. Chips of plaster and brick flew into his face, stinging his cheek. He flinched back, and his heels jammed back against the step behind him, and he went down on his backside, a fucking sitting duck he thought. But one of his colleagues, named Dirk he remembered, fired two quick shots, and Dyatlov saw another robed figure slump to the floor at the bottom.

While he was picking himself up Dirk dashed down into the shadows, and then reappeared seconds later.

"Clear!" he shouted.

Dyatlov joined him with the third team-member. "Thanks," he mumbled quietly.

The three of them stepped through another open door, this one disguised to look like a brick wall, and stopped. They were at the end of yet another passage. To their left part of the ceiling had come down, spilling wooden joists onto the floor. Beyond this was a curtained partition. Immediately to their right, a heavy iron door, partially ajar. Dyatlov lifted two fingers and pointed left. He went through the iron door on his own.

Several burning torches laying on the stone floor flared brightly through his night-vision goggles, nearly blinding him, so he lifted them up onto his forehead and blinked rapidly to clear his sight. Arranged in a circle were about a dozen chairs, and he saw the corpse seated in one, its slumped posture giving it an obscene appearance. Dyatlov stepped forward for a closer look, and saw just how old it was, the bones and skull and ragged garments looking all dry and dusty.

The room was small. In one wall, several feet above the surface of the floor, was a tiny square opening, like the mouth of a tunnel. Other than the old corpse the place was unoccupied, and Dyatlov was about to turn away and re-join his men when the sound of splashing water reached his ears, above the din of battle overhead.

He turned back, and then noticed the circular pit in the floor, which he now saw was filling with water.

Crouching forward for a better view, he was shocked to see a man chained up beneath the surface, kicking and grappling with his bonds, and by the looks of it, about to breathe his last gasp. He was further dismayed when he recognized the person.

"Holy fucking Christ!" he blurted out.

What the heck was Van Dijk doing here? And more to the point, was he too late to get him out?

Dyatlov leaped down into the hole and rammed his hand into the water to grab the Inspector by the front of his jacket, then heaved upwards. Which was silly. The policeman wasn't going anywhere tied up like this. So he looked around in desperation, his eyes quickly falling on the metal plate near his shoes. Slipping his finger through the ring, he again heaved upwards, and lifted the heavy plate clear, and the water immediately started to drain away, the level dropping quickly. Van Dijk's face came clear as the pit emptied, and he was coughing and puking up water, and looking very blue as he inhaled huge mouthfuls of air.

"This is no time to be having a bath Van Dijk. Stay there, I'll find something to break those chains." He grinned from ear to ear, looking like a madman no doubt.

"I'm not going anywhere Dyatlov."

Racing out into the passage, the assault leader rooted about amidst the wreckage from the collapsed ceiling and came up with a short length of iron pipe. Rushing back through the doorway he used it to twist and turn at the manacles locked around Van Dijk's wrists and ankles, eventually snapping them open. He helped the Inspector out of the pit. He stood there dripping wet, but at least he looked to have recovered his breathing and his strength.

"You took your damn time getting here," he said as he straightened up.

"You should thank Adolf. He was the one who finally found out about them using this place."

Somewhere above them the firefight seemed to be intensifying, the building shaking again as more explosive blasts rumbled the walls.

Pieter nodded at the ceiling. "How are we doing?"

"It's a fucking nightmare. This place is like a fucking maze." As he answered, he flicked a switch and spoke into his comms mike. "Black Team, Red here. Give me a fucking update."

He listened to the response in his ear-piece, leaving Pieter waiting.

"Ok, we're clear down here... I think. Hold them at the top, we'll link up." He turned back to Pieter. "It's a warzone up there, worse than yesterday. But it looks like we have the final few pinned down and cornered right at the top." He reached into his body armour and pulled out a handgun, then offered it to Pieter, along with a couple of spare clips. "We could do with all the help we can get."

Pieter took the proffered weapon. Before they moved out he pointed at the tiny tunnel entrance behind them. "You might want to leave someone covering that. It's a way in and out."

"Yes, I wondered about that. Whoever is in charge of this bunch, they were fucking well prepared."

Pieter grinned an unpleasant grin. "Oh I know who's running the show. And they're fucking mine."

"Be my guest. What about through the curtain down the corridor? What's in there?"

Pieter told him briefly, about the catacombs, and the crazy ceremony, and of course Officer Joos. This last bit made Dyatlov wince. He patted Pieter on the shoulder.

"Don't worry. The bastards aren't getting away this time."

It soon became clear that Lotte's deranged followers had no intention of trying to escape. Their fanaticism and total obedience was absolute, and they fought tooth and nail for every room and staircase, every landing and corridor and square foot of ground, regardless of the cost to them. Perhaps they had been pumped full of drugs or maybe they were just utterly brainwashed. Whatever the case, surrender was not an option for them. So it fell to Dyatlov and his men, with Pieter's help, to prise them out and neutralize them one by one.

In the large room containing Officer Joos' butchered remains, hidden at the back of one of the archways, they quickly located another staircase, this one leading upwards. They followed it up, heading towards the sound of gunfire.

Signs of fighting were everywhere, the wood-panelled walls and balustrade splintered with gunshot and grenade. On one landing they stepped over another masked corpse still gripping on to its assault rifle. A little further up, another body sitting slumped over, again dressed in those sinister dark robes. From the looks of it he had ripped away his wood-carved mask and taken his own life by placing a handgun into his mouth and pulling the trigger.

191

Smoke was everywhere, catching in the back of Pieter's throat, and his eyes watered from the tear gas, but he pushed on just behind Dyatlov.

Over his comms suite Dyatlov was informed that the last of the holdouts were now contained on the upper landing. They reached the spot moments later, amid the fierce firefight taking place.

One end of the hallway was occupied by members of Black and Red Team, the other by a handful of the enemy. Every now and then a robed gunman would pop out from a doorway and fire towards the police, and the police would respond in kind.

Pieter hung back, realizing this was a job for the professionals, and he found himself wondering if Lotte was amongst the group still holding out. Most likely she was. He listened as Dyatlov issued a series of instructions to his men. Enough was enough, it was time to end this, he told them. At his command they would fill the far end of the hallway with as much gunfire as possible together with stun grenades, tear gas and concussion grenades. They would use maximum force. If they wanted to die like crazy fanatics, then they would grant them their wish.

Pieter moved away and sheltered behind a nearby corner, hunkering down as much as possible, and braced himself.

When it came the cacophony of noise was frightful. The sound of sustained machine-gun fire, accompanied by a series of violent explosions, ripped apart his world and sucked the air from his lungs. His ears rang like bells in a church tower, and the dust made him cough and splutter, and he lay flat on the floor, and prayed that the building would not split apart.

Slowly a strange hush settled and Pieter pushed himself to his feet, brushing dust from his hair and face. He waited a moment, hoping it was over. Then he heard voices, a few muttered words and then a nervous laugh, and he relaxed.

It was done.

From further down the landing by the end wall, Bart watched him through the smoke.

During the fighting, he'd sustained a nasty wound to his scalp, and his face was a mask of red blood. His clothes were torn, and his knuckles were raw from fighting with one of the policemen. He'd lost his gun at some stage and instead had scooped up one of the scythes somebody had dropped onto the floor. Now he stood there, still and silent, with the weapon in his hand and a fury bubbling deep inside, hating this man with a cold fury at what he'd done, the way this interfering fool had wrecked their plans, their years of careful preparations.

They should have killed him weeks ago, months ago, just like Bart had said. It was too dangerous having a police officer, the main homicide detective investigating their crimes, so near to the heart of their plans. Yet Lotte had insisted, saying she had everything worked out, that all of the pieces were slipping perfectly into place exactly as she had predicted. So he had gone along with it, trusting her judgement. Totally devoted to her as he was.

Yet it had all fallen apart. Something, somewhere, had gone wrong. Perhaps his sister's abilities in the dark arts were not as refined as she thought, in spite of the things he had seen her do, the wonderful feats she had performed.

Maybe, just maybe, her feelings for the cop had been her undoing.

Because of that everything was over, their schemes lay in ruins, with most of their followers dead.

There was still time to put one thing right though. It would not alter the eventual outcome, but it would be a fitting way to exact revenge.

Lifting the scythe and gripping it in both hands Bart charged at the cop, screaming his hatred.

Pieter heard the heavy footsteps and then the loud yell, which shattered the stillness. He spun in alarm, and saw the huge figure racing towards him, instantly recognizing Bart, and then registering the wicked-looking blade of the scythe swinging straight towards his head.

He pulled up his pistol and fired at nearly point-blank range, three rapid shots, all of them finding their target and thudding into Bart's huge bulk. Bart stumbled slightly, then carried on running, the momentum of his charge propelling him forward, and Pieter's fourth shot hit him in the throat, and this time he saw him stagger, and a look of shock was etched over the other man's face as his strength gave way and he went crashing down to the floor, losing his grip on the scythe, which sliced straight through his chest as he landed on it, until the blade burst out of his back.

Pieter jumped away and stared down at Bart.

He watched him draw in two deep breaths, which sounded more like a wheezing death rattle, and turn his face to stare up at Pieter, his eyes twin holes of smouldering hate.

Then with one last grunt his body sagged.

Shortly after a heavy and cloying stench of burning drifted up the staircase, and within minutes the upper landing was filling with dense, black clouds of smoke. A hurried conversation took place between Dyatlov and his other team leaders, who were positioned at different locations throughout the huge building. News soon spread. There was a fire down in the catacombs, probably started accidentally during the gun and grenade battle, and it was spreading fast.

So it was time to get out.

Grabbing their dead and wounded, the various members of each assault team started to evacuate the building. Nobody bothered about removing the corpses of the robed and masked gunmen and gunwomen: they could burn in hell for all anybody cared. Anyway, speed was of the essence.

On the way down Pieter came across Famke's body.

He'd lost track of her amidst all of the mayhem, and it was impossible to tell one masked person from another anyway. As it was, he only spotted her now by chance.

He and other men from Dyatlov's unit were hurrying down the stairs when they passed by a small room just off one short hallway, and Pieter just happened to glance into the doorway. He stopped dead and then doubled back, letting the others squeeze by, then he ducked inside.

194

Her body lay with a group of three other corpses. The room was riddled with bullet holes and the floor covered with brass cartridge cases, and a heavy smell of cordite permeated the air. Their robes and skin had been torn and ripped in a grenade blast, but Famke's face was untouched, and her eyes stared sightlessly up at the ceiling. In her hand she held her mask, having removed it in her final moments.

Pieter stood there, remembering her cruel words as she had gloated over killing his dad, and something sharp stabbed his heart, a mixture of pity, anger and betrayal. There was also a sense of guilt, which he knew was unjustifiable. Nevertheless, he wondered yet again if he had been stupid and naïve to fall for all of Famke's and Lotte's lies and deceptions.

There would be time to answer these doubts later. Time to face up to and work through his anguish.

He turned away and shut the door.

Let them burn. Let them all burn.

The fire consumed the whole building, and it soon became a raging inferno that lit up the city skyline for miles around.

Out on the market square dozens of onlookers gathered to watch the famous landmark burn to the ground. All of Dyatlov's men had been accounted for, all of their deceased and injured carried out, and those that could be saved were whisked away by ambulance. Fire crews arrived but it was deemed too dangerous for them to approach and tackle the blaze because of all of the unexploded ordnance still inside. Besides, it felt fitting just to leave it to burn itself out.

Standing there with the others, Pieter watched the flames soar into the night sky, and his eyes followed the multitude of burning embers drift up towards the bright moon overhead.

He thought about Lotte.

Reduced to ashes with the rest.

Pieter nodded silently to himself.

CHAPTER 21

FOUR MONTHS LATER

L eaving the small guest house, Pieter crossed over the main promenade road and started walking along the coastal path through the sand dunes.

A stiff breeze blew in off the North Sea, and he stood at the top of one grassy hummock looking out at the waves rolling in to the shore. It was early, a little before seven in the morning, and the air had that early-autumn chill, but it looked set to be a crisp and clear day. The kind of day that blew away the cobwebs and invigorated him.

He set off along the sandy beach.

Back in the spring Pieter had been ordered to take a long sabbatical, by his bosses in the Amsterdam Police and also by his shrink. They'd told him he needed time to readjust, to touch base with life again, and all of that crap. What they'd really meant was that he should go away and let himself heal, and not to return until he was ready.

So he had done as they suggested. He had escaped from the city for a while, and come here, to the pretty town of Katwijk aan Zee, to enjoy the sea air and admire the views, to soak up some healthy ozone amidst the quaint little houses with their red-tiled roofs and the fancy cobbled streets.

He'd booked into a small guest house run by two middle-aged men and payed in cash on a week-by-week basis, and he had easily slipped into a new routine.

Each morning he would rise early and go for a brisk walk along the beach or through the sand dunes, and then double back to the main coast road and circle back to the guest house, perhaps buying a daily newspaper along the way. Then he would enjoy breakfast – toast with marmalade followed by two hard-boiled-eggs – and then sit in one of the wicker chairs in the glass-roofed veranda and watch the world go by. After lunch, weather permitting, he might take an amble along to the yacht marina or maybe down to Katwijk Lighthouse where he would admire the views from the top, or if he fancied a longer hike he would set off southwards along the beach where the coast was quieter, and just keep walking and soaking up the peace and quiet of the open air. He would sit on the sand and eat the packed-lunch that the guest house owners would make up for him, and think a little, but mostly just watch the gulls swoop through the strong offshore winds. Then later in the afternoon, he would catch the bus back and watch a little TV in the lounge.

He caught little bits of the news regarding events back in Amsterdam, but he tried not to immerse himself in the details too much. Suffice it to say that the city, the whole nation actually, was still coming to terms with events.

The shock was wearing off and now people were asking serious questions about just what exactly had been going on. The police were typically tight-lipped, but mostly because they didn't really know much themselves. They desperately tried to play down the more weird and bizarre aspects of the case, denying the rumours of an occult sect, which they described as hocus-pocus nonsense! Instead they stuck to the bare facts: that the murders had stopped, the killers were dead, the police force and public had paid a heavy price in the number of casualties, but the most important thing was that it was over.

But what about the murderers? People asked. Just who were they?

And that was part of the problem.

Of all of the bodies removed from the burnt out shell that was The Waag, together with those killed during the attack at Schreierstoren Tower, which in total numbered around about forty dead, so far only a handful had been identified. Many had been burned beyond recognition, sure, but still, it was expected that through DNA and dental records they should have been able to ID the vast majority of them. But the simple fact was that very few of them were in the police database, either in The Netherlands or abroad. They were not in the system at all. They were known as clean skins, and finding out who exactly they were might prove impossible. They might never know who these murderous fanatics or their leaders were.

It was one huge mess.

Pieter was glad to be out of the loop.

He arrived back at the guest house just after eight and went straight through to the breakfast area, where he enjoyed a quick hello and chat with Ruben and Max, before they left him to tuck in. The radio was on quietly and he caught the weather forecast: clear skies but with stiff and cold breezes, before a low front moved in later. Maybe he would catch the bus south and then walk back, just for a change. If he got caught in any showers then he didn't mind that, it would be fun in a way.

Finished eating, he headed back up to his room to grab a few things, passing another guest on the stairs, a young lady wearing a baseball hat. She smiled and then slipped by, and he heard the front door click shut.

Pieter unlocked his room door, and walked in. Then stopped dead.

He looked across at his bed, and the small object lying on top of his pillow.

With his heart hammering in his chest, he walked slowly across. He felt his shoes crunching over something on the carpet, which made him pause and look down at the soil there, and even as he saw this, and picked up the small ring with its familiar skull on the front, he understood.

Pieter flew across the room to the only window and looked out.

And there she was. Standing on the pavement across the street, with the dunes and the sea behind her. The lady in the hat. Looking up at him, and smiling.

But a bus went by then, blocking his view of her, and once it had gone past, he knew, he just knew!

Lotte was gone.

Pieter raised the flat of his hand against the glass and banged it over and over in frustration.

He looked left and right up and down the street.

She was nowhere to be seen.

AUTHOR'S NOTE

This is of course a work of fiction, but some parts of it are based on actual events:

Unternehmen Werwolf – Operation Werewolf was the brainchild of SS Obergruppenfuhrer Hans-Adolf Prutzmann, General Inspector of Special Defence. Under orders from Reichsfuhrer Heinrich Himmler to create a special commando unit of highly-trained operatives whose role would be to remain back behind enemy lines as occupied Europe was liberated by Allied forces, he came up with the Werewolf Commando Force. Their members were mostly made up of young men and teenagers from the Hitler Youth or young ladies from the BDM – The League of German Girls. Hulchrath Castle was their main training camp. Here they took part in map-reading, rifle practice, first-aid techniques, boxing and wrestling, hand-to-hand combat, preparation for acts of sabotage such as making mines from empty tins of Heinz soup, and learning assassination skills.

Operation Carnival likewise was a real operation. The members of the team, led by Herbert Wenzel, were tasked with assassinating the Mayor of Aachen, Franz Oppenhoff. The mission was pretty much as I have described in the novel, and all of the hit-squad members in my story were real people, including the young She-Wolf Ilse Hirsch. After the operation, Wenzel disappeared without trace, presumably spending the rest of his life living under a new identity. Although the surviving members of the hit-squad were rounded up and arrested shortly after the war, all were found not guilty and released. Hirsch lived to a ripe old age.

Radio Werewolf was part of Joseph Goebbels propaganda machine. The broadcasts were intended both to boost the morale of the Wehrmacht and the German population, as well as to instil fear amongst the Allied troops.

All of the locations that I have used throughout the story are real places, and many are worth a visit:

Schreierstoren Tower (or Weeping Tower) and The Waag are currently very pleasant cafes and bars, and patrons are always made to feel very welcome: alas, there are no robed or masked occult followers waiting to pounce on you! The Nemo Science Museum is a fantastic place to take your children, while the rooftop terrace where my chase sequence comes to a dramatic end, is completely free to visit – and the views across Amsterdam are simply breathtaking.

There is no secret tunnel between The Newcastle Bar and The Waag, however there is one underneath Bar Papeneiland. Just ask the bartender to point out the entrance underneath the steps. It dates back to a time when Catholicism was illegal in Holland, and Catholics would often meet in secret churches. The tunnel here led to one such secret church, which is sadly now demollshed. For the novel I simply relocated this tunnel to Thc Newcastle Bar (another lovely drinking spot – the bar staff are not at all surly like Bart)

Amsterdam's Red Light District needs no introduction. It is one of the city's main tourist attractions, and is surprisingly very safe to visit, even late at night. It is well policed and most petty crimes are stamped upon quite harshly by the city authorities (not literally, as may have once been the case.) Please respect the working girls, and photography is strictly forbidden. If you follow the rules, the pimps and enforcers will leave you alone. If you don't, you may very well end up in one of the canals.

There is a small convent in the village of Koningsbosch. Access inside is understandably carefully managed as it is a private and secluded place of worship. Both the convent and the village are beautiful, and the locals very friendly (and I'm sure the nuns are too)

Finally, the last location in the story, Katwijk aan Zee, is a gorgeous seaside town overlooking the North Sea. The beaches are pristine and the air full of healthy ozone. But be warned – Lotte may still be lurking!!

Mark Hobson
March 2020 – October 2020

ABOUT THE AUTHOR

Mark Hobson is a writer and historian. His works span numerous genres from military history to thrillers and horror, both fiction and non-fiction.

He lives at home in Yorkshire with his 3 cats.

Wolf Angel is Book 1 in The Amsterdam Occult Series.

His previous works include:

Now May Men Weep – Isandlwana: A Story From the Zulu War.
Ntombe 1879 (Non-fiction)
Isandlwana – A Military Enigma (Non-fiction)

Wolf Angel

Mark Hobson

Mark Hobson

Printed in Poland
by Amazon Fulfillment
Poland Sp. z o.o., Wrocław